Oliver's Gift

Marjorie Bocking

AN M-Y BOOKS PAPERBACK

A CIP catalogue record for this title is
available from the British Library

ISBN– 978-1-909908-93-2

*To Stephanie for all her help and kindness
without which this book would
never have been published.*

*Also to Jean who encouraged me to put
pencil to paper in the first place.*

To Phillis + Brian
with my love
MB
To
Marjorie Botting

iii

Acknowledgements:

Many thanks to Elizabeth and James at BookCreateService for all their support and patience and to Linda Elder for her excellent proofreading and helpful comments.

Part One

It all began when my Australian cousin came to stay.

Caiti had decided to discover Norfolk – as she put it! After hearing so much about it from her great grandparents, it had become Caiti's ambition to visit one day. Now here she was, blonde, beautiful with boundless energy and always ready for anything. In the month Caiti has been staying with my husband Jim and me, we have seen and done things in Norfolk that we had not done in all our thirty plus years together. We have been on the Ghost Walk in King's Lynn (Caiti says she is psychic!), collected cockles at Snettisham, crabs at Cromer and been over to Seal Island from Blakeney. We have sailed on the Broads and eaten bloaters in Yarmouth. Now after two days exploring Norwich Caiti has decided it is time to move on again.

"I want to see the little villages Granpop told me about," she'd stated. "Let's just drive into the countryside and see what turns up."

So there we were, completely lost in deepest Norfolk! The signposts were few and far between but Caiti was enthralled.

"That looks like a nice little road," she'd say. "Turn down there Jim."

Jim did as bidden! I must admit I was enjoying the scenery. The hedgerows were ablaze with colour. Wild roses and honeysuckle entangled in the lush green of the blackthorn hedges, foxgloves standing like sentinels, patches of dainty blue hare-bells and scabious interspersed with the yellow of toadflax and the pink of campions. Norfolk was certainly at its best today, I mused.

"That looks like a village up ahead," said Jim suddenly. "We'd better stop and fill up the petrol tank."

"And my tummy, I'm starving!" said Caiti. Jim and I laughed. We'd noticed that she was fond of her food.

The village, when we arrived, was very pretty though not very big. A smallish Saxon church stood in its graveyard almost hidden by elderly trees. The church roof was thatched as were some of the cottages which lined the village green. A few ducks waddled across the green though I could see no pond, just swings and slides for the children. Jim parked the car by the side of the green and we all climbed out to stretch our legs. The ducks came hurrying towards us evidently thinking a meal was forthcoming!

"Sorry Donald," laughed Jim as a particularly noisy drake began tugging at his sleeve. "If we can find a shop or somewhere that sells bread you can have some later."

"Is that a pub over there?" asked Caiti. Jim and I looked in the direction she was pointing.

"Looks like it, although I can't see a sign," I said.

We started off over the green to investigate. The ducks, realising they were not getting fed, waddled away in the direction of the church. As we neared the building which we guessed must be the village inn, we could see a sign propped up against a door. A door, which like the rest of the building, needed a coat of paint. White paint was peeling from the walls and the window frames and sills looked quite rotten. Yet for all its forlorn appearance there was something very homely and welcoming about it.

"*Riverside Inn*" we read on the sign. "Food hot or cold. Coaches welcome."

"Oh good!" said Caiti who ducked under the arch of roses hanging over the low door and entered.

Inside, the inn was just as I thought it would be. Low oak beamed ceilings, white uneven walls and a large inglenook fireplace complete with spit and shiny brass fire irons. A collection of martingales decorated the oak mantelpiece and in the fireplace itself stood a large arrangement of dried flowers and grasses. To the right of the fireplace was a small bar with a door behind it, obviously leading to the living quarters. In front, but slightly to the right of the bar, two elderly men sat playing dominoes. Other than glancing at us when we entered they took no further notice and carried on with their game. We stood in the room for several moments gazing around at the pictures which adorned the walls. Most were modern country scenes but a few seemed quite old. I could see that Caiti was impressed – she being an artist herself.

"I wonder who F.F. is?" she remarked, studying a signature at the bottom of one of the landscapes. Just then a door at the back of the room opened and a young man entered. Time stood still as Caiti and the man looked at each other. I could almost feel the electricity that was sparking between them. Even the two old domino players looked up. Then Jim broke the tension by saying "Would you be the landlord, Mr. Er-?"

"Fullerton – Tom Fullerton," he answered, extending his hand to Jim. "Actually, my mother is the landlady, but she's gone off to Norwich for the day since business is rather slack. But you don't want to hear about our troubles. What can I get you?"

Suddenly Caiti found her voice.

"It says on your board that you do meals. Can you rustle something up for us please – oh, and why is this place called the *Riverside Inn*? We didn't see a river."

Tom Fullerton laughed, showing strong white teeth. His attractive face was tanned as if he spent a great deal of time outside and his hair was the most amazing colour - a kind of red gold that looked as if it was on fire when a shaft of sunlight caught it as he stood by the window.

"I'll answer your questions separately," he said, going to a door behind the bar. Opening the door he called "Fiona, can you come a moment – we have customers." We heard footsteps and then a slim, attractive girl appeared.

"I'm sorry," she said, "I never heard you come in. What can I do for you?"

"Could we have a 'light' lunch please?" I asked, as Caiti, still gazing at Tom, seemed to have been struck dumb. Tom dragged his dark blue eyes away from Caiti's green ones and reached for a menu which was on the bar.

"Oh," he said, handing me a menu, "I'm forgetting my manners. This is Fiona Fullerton. Chef Extraordinaire! We couldn't do without her." Caiti's face dropped. I could see what she was thinking. "So this gorgeous man is married. Just my luck!"

We studied the menu and found that all the dishes were Norfolk orientated. It being too hot for dumplings, we settled on samphire with brown bread and butter for starters, followed by roast lamb with new potatoes and fresh garden peas, with Norfolk vinegar cake to finish.

"Would you care for a drink while you're waiting?" Fiona asked.

"Not for me!" Jim indicated Caiti and me. "No reason why you shouldn't though." We chose to have a long cold glass of lager.

"If you'd like to follow me," Tom smiled, "I'll show you the river."

Picking up our drinks, we followed him through the door by which he'd entered, and passed through a room which was obviously the dining room and out through a large glass door onto a wide patio. There were tables and chairs with bright umbrellas and pots of geraniums placed about, and there was the river, or rather a wide stream, shimmering in the sunlight, most of it to our left almost hidden by weeping willows. It formed a 'U' with the inn situated at the bottom and the right arm curving away into the distance.

"Wow, cool," breathed Caiti as she ran across the patio and onto the river bank. "This is just so English, just like Granpop described his Norfolk villages. Somehow I feel at home, almost as if I've been here before."

Tom laughed.

"Perhaps you have," he said, "in a previous life".

"Oh I do wish I could throw off my clothes and have a swim," Caiti said.

"Don't you dare," I said quickly, knowing her impetuous nature.

"Would a boat trip do instead?" asked Tom. "We have time for a quick row before your lunch if you'd care to. My boat is in the willows."

"I'd love to," said Caiti "but wouldn't your wife mind?"

Tom threw back his red gold head and rocked with mirth.

"Wife," he choked. "I don't have a wife." Caiti stared at him, her face getting pinker by the second.

"But- but I thought Fiona was...." she tailed off embarrassed.

"Fiona is my sister, I should have explained."

"In that case lead me to the boat, wherever it is," Caiti beamed.

Tom began to walk towards the willow trees then suddenly turned about to face Jim and I.

"There's room for you too," he said.

"I think Meg and I will stay here and enjoy the view, thanks all the same," Jim said and I saw a twinkle in his eye. It was obvious that they would prefer to be alone. With a quick wave they were gone and then we heard the splash of oars in the water and Caiti's silvery laugh getting fainter and fainter into the distance. Jim leaned back in one of the patio chairs.

"How's that for love at first sight?" he said. "During all the time Caiti has been with us she's shown no interest in men at all, now she's well and truly smitten."

I agreed and settled back to enjoy my drink. The day was so perfect and the scenery so beautiful. Butterflies of several varieties were sipping nectar from a buddleia bush in the garden and fat bumble bees droned amongst the roses. It was all so peaceful that I closed my eyes and the next thing I knew Fiona was calling us in for our lunch.

"I've set a table for you in the dining room," she said. "You won't get pestered by flies in there, but you can still see the river."

We thanked her and followed her into a room which, like the bar, had paintings on the wall. Then something in my brain clicked.

"F.F.!" I exclaimed. "You must be the artist."

Fiona blushingly admitted it.

"Do you sell them?" Jim wanted to know.

"Occasionally," she said. "I just do it for fun really." Then we heard voices and Caiti and Tom appeared in the doorway.

"Just in time," I said, smiling at Caiti's smug little face.

"I'd better see if Fiona needs any help," said Tom to us, although his eyes never left Caiti. Then he turned and disappeared into the bar. Caiti sighed.

"Must go and freshen up," she said, "I've had such a lovely time."

She headed for a door marked 'Ladies' and returned just as Fiona brought in our samphire with brown bread and butter.

Throughout our so called 'light lunch' we were regaled with how marvellous Tom was, how handsome etc. etc.

"He's a farmer really," Caiti told us. "His father owns all the land around here and even the village itself. Tom was studying for a degree in law at Uni. but then his father had a bad accident which left him with a crippled leg, so Tom left Uni. and came home to help run the farm. He's offered to show us around this afternoon if we can stay on for a while. We can, can't we? Oh do say we can." How Caiti managed to eat her lunch and talk as well I really do not know.

"Can we?" she asked again. Jim and I looked at her radiant face and neither of us had the heart to refuse.

"We can spare a couple of hours, and then we really must be on our way," Jim told her.

Fiona came to clear away the plates and Tom followed her in, bringing with him a tray laden with cups and a coffee pot.

"You must sit down and join us," invited Jim. "Tell us about your farm. You must be very hard pressed to run it and the inn."

Tom and Fiona sat down and I poured out the coffee.

"He won't tell you, but I will," said Fiona. "It's extremely hard on him – on us all really. Father and Paul, that's our younger brother, run the farm between them but we have to muck in when things get extra busy. Tom is there most of the time but has to be here a lot too. Mum spends most of the day here, just going home at night and sometimes for only an hour or two to clean and cook."

"Do you live here then?" I asked. Fiona nodded. "Yes, but I do have a friend who has a room here, so I'm not on my own exactly. Jean works in Wymondham during the day and then fills in as a barmaid when she gets home. My boyfriend gets called in to help too when we have a darts match or something. We used to get coaches stopping for refreshments until the by-pass was built. Now we are cut off and becoming a forgotten village."

Tom and Caiti had been chatting quietly during Fiona's monologue, now Tom looked up.

"You must have noticed how run-down everything is," he said. "We just haven't had the money to do all the repairs. The farm is only just paying its way. If we have a little profit then we spend it doing up one of the cottages, then one of the farm machines packs up and we're back to square one."

"Couldn't you sell the cottages to the sitting tenants?" Jim asked.

Tom sadly shook his head.

"Most of the villagers are elderly and I know they couldn't afford to buy their cottages and we couldn't just give them notice to leave. They do help by providing us with fresh vegetables though. And with the rent they pay we can just make ends meet."

"The lamb we've just eaten was delicious," I said. "Was that local too?"

Fiona nodded.

"Everything we use is mostly from the farm. We keep a cow or two, some pigs and chickens and about fifty sheep."

"Goodness," I exclaimed, "you must be worn out by the end of the day. When do you find time for a bit of recreation Tom?"

"I don't," he laughed, "that's how I've got to be twenty-eight and unmarried. I did ask one girl if I could take her to the pictures, but then a ewe decided to lamb early and I couldn't leave it, so she dumped me and that was the end of that! Anyway you didn't come here to listen to our moans. If you've finished your coffee we'd better be on our way to the farm. That's if you'd like to," he added.

"We'd love to," answered Jim and I together, and Caiti's face was one large beam. Together we walked through into the bar where Jim took out his debit card and paid for our meal. "Is there anywhere in the village where we can buy petrol?" he asked, "our tank is nearly on empty."

Tom shook his head.

" 'fraid not. The nearest garage is about six miles away. I could let you have can full to help you get there."

"That would be very kind of you," said Jim, "which direction would it be in?"

Tom looked out of the window to see which way our car was facing.

"That's good," he said "if you follow the green to the end, turn left, you will find the road follows the river for a while, then you take the next turn right. The road is called Primrose Lane. It will take you to the next village."

"Dunt yew goo down thet there road!"

We turned to see the two old men we had seen earlier. They had just come in from the outside door. Been home for their midday meal, I guessed.

"Why not?" asked Jim.

" 'Aunted, " they replied, and chuckling they sat down and began another game of dominoes. Laughing, Tom led us outside.

"That's Joe and Ted," he informed us. "They used to work on the farm once. Since they've retired they come into the inn for company. Both of them have lost their wives so it's something for them to do. When their 'screws' are not playing them up they help by keeping our garden in order and Fiona slips them a meal most days."

We followed Tom to a battered Landrover parked by the side of the inn and climbed in. Caiti, of course, made sure that she was sitting in front with Tom. We set off for the farm, following the left side of the river which meandered its merry way along through clumps of bulrushes and reeds. Once I thought I caught a glimpse of a kingfisher. It was certainly pretty. Gazing enthralled at the river, I had not seen anything of the other side of the road until the Landrover came to a halt outside a gate. The gate was open, hanging crookedly on its hinges. Across the top was a metal bar which bore the words 'Oliver's Gift'.

Caiti turned to Tom. "Is that the name of the farm?"

"It is," he said.

We looked about us. Whoever needed to go abroad when there was all this beauty here in Norfolk I thought to myself.

"Who's Oliver?" asked Caiti.

"Don't be inquisitive Caiti," I chided.

Tom laughed and put a brown muscular arm around my young cousin. "I don't mind her asking questions. She's like a breath of spring to me. To answer your question Caiti, I'm afraid I can't tell you. The name goes back many generations. There have always been Fullertons here for as long as we can trace back. There are some tomb- stones in the church yard dating from the 1600s but there is nothing that explains who Oliver was and why he left it to us."

As he spoke Tom began to drive through the gate and along a rough track which eventually came to a group of farm buildings. Chickens ran to us and then they were scattered as a black and white Border Collie bitch and her puppy ran to meet us, barking joyfully. Tom opened his door and ran round to help Caiti alight. With an amused smile Jim rushed round and opened my door sweeping an extra regal bow as he did so.

"This is the working part of the farm," Tom told us, leading us into the first barn, all clean and swept out ready for the grain harvest which we knew would be ready in a few weeks. The next building housed the combine harvester and a couple of tractors. We toured the rest of the buildings including cow sheds and a sparkling sterile dairy. Then Tom led us through a cobbled yard and at last we saw the house.

"Wow!" breathed Caiti. "It's beautiful. No wonder you love it."

The house stood on a slight incline, overlooking the river

which now formed an ox-bow. Behind the house, fields of ripening corn and bright yellow rape oil seed contrasted with the rich lushness of the meadows and river bank. Sheep were grazing lazily in the heat of the day and walking among them was a man who, even from a distance, looked like an older edition of Tom.

"Looks as if Dad is checking out the sheep, some will have to go to market next week," Tom said. "Come along into the house and have a cup of tea. Dad will be in shortly."

Jim and I started to follow him towards the house. It looked as if it had had extensions added to it over the years, but the original building was definitely Tudor. 'Very interesting,' I thought. Then realising Caiti was not with us I turned to look for her. She was standing on the top of the incline with her hands holding her head, staring into the distance, not realising what an attractive picture she made with her pale green dress billowing gently around her shapely legs, her long blonde hair hanging to her waist.

"What are you looking at Caiti?" I called.

"There is something missing," she said without turning.

"What do you mean?"

"That tree way back there. It just isn't right."

"Caiti, don't be silly. You haven't been here before."

"I have. I know I have." Caiti turned slowly and joined me, her face still puzzled. Her green eyes looked glazed almost as if she was in a trance, her face ashen white. Shaking her gently I waited until her colour returned, then led her into the house. The men were busy in the kitchen, rattling cups etc. They looked up as we entered.

"We thought you were lost," said Tom grinning.

"Just looking at the scenery," I said hastily.

Tom indicated the chairs around a well-scrubbed table and we all sat down, to be joined moments later by Tom's father. Tom introduced us to the older man and we found that he, also, was named Tom.

"Every first born son in this family is christened Tom. Goes

12

back as far as we can track," he told us. The two dogs had come into the kitchen and were being fussed over by Caiti.

"What are their names?" she asked Tom senior.

"Jess is the mother," she was told, " but so far we haven't thought of a name for her puppy. Perhaps you'd like to name him for us?" Caiti flung her arms around the little dog who gave her face an ecstatic washing, its little body wriggling excitedly.

"It's got to be Benjy," she told us, "after my dog at home in Australia."

"That's it then," agreed the two Toms. Tom the younger took Caiti's hand and led her to the door. "You obviously love animals," he said. "Come and see the kittens in the barn. They haven't opened their eyes yet." So saying, he led Caiti into the yard and across to a large thatched barn, the two dogs bounding around them as they went.

Tom senior watched them go, and then turned to us with a grin on his weather-beaten face.

"He's certainly taken with young Caiti," he said, "never seen him looking so love-struck." Jim and I laughed.

"Love at first sight for them both I suspect," I said,

"but she's due to fly back home at the end of the month, so what happens then?"

"The phone will be red-hot I expect," laughed Tom senior, just as a battered blue Fiesta car pulled into the yard. "Ah, here's the missus. I'm glad you haven't missed her."

Marie Fullerton came into the house. She was a plump, smartly dressed woman with brown wavy hair just beginning to turn grey. Kicking off her shoes, she flexed her toes.

"Dratted shoes," she muttered, "they don't half give me gyp."

Tom chuckled. "You should have worn your trainers," he said. Then he gently turned her around so that she was facing us. "Look," he added, "we have visitors."

Marie's attractive face turned bright red.

"Oh, I do beg your pardon. Whatever must you think of me?"

"Think nothing of it," I assured her. "I have a pair at home which nip me if I walk very far in them."

Tom was busy doing the introductions when in walked young Tom and Caiti.

"And this is Caiti," Tom said crossing the room to his mother. "Isn't she beautiful?"

"Hello Caiti," greeted Marie. "Short for Catherine is it?"

"No, Mrs Fullerton, it's really Caitlin. I think my mother was reading a novel whose heroine was called Caitlin, so when I was born I got stuck with it."

"Well it's a beautiful name and as Tom says, you are a beautiful girl. Your parents must be very proud of you."

Caiti shook her head. "I never knew my mother. She died in a plane crash when I was two and my Dad died of some kind of fever when I was ten. I've lived with my Uncle and Aunt ever since."

"Oh my dear, I'm so terribly sorry, me and my big mouth. Tom says I'm always putting my foot in it."

Caiti gave her a quick hug. "Don't worry about it. It all happened a long time ago."

"I don't want to spoil the party," broke in Jim, "but we really must get going. We have to collect the petrol and refuel the car yet. It'll be getting dark by the time we get home."

Back at the village we bade a quick farewell to Fiona and walked across the green to our car, accompanied by young Tom. Whilst the men, watched by Caiti, were tipping in the petrol, I walked across the green to where I could see the two old gents we had met earlier that day. They were sitting on a wooden bench overlooking the children's play area.

"Hello again," I said. "Is it always as quiet as this?" Joe – or was it Ted? – lifted rheumy eyes to mine.

"Moost the toime," he replied. "Though we did hev a car stop laast week. Blook stuck 'is 'ed outer winder. He say, all la de da loike, 'Can yer tell me the quickest way ter git ter Fairkenham?' Well I scratched ma 'hid and thort a bit, cus since they put in thet ole by-pass an' altered a lot of the roods thas not so easy. Well 'ee statted giteen aireated. 'Come on man,' he say, 'Do you know or not?' Well I say I can't roightly

14

say. 'You're a fule,' he say all bigoty loike. 'Ah,' I say, 'I might be a fule but I hent lorst.'"

With this the two old men doffed their greasy caps and made off towards the inn, chortling as they went, and I turned back to join the others who were saying their farewells.

"I'll ring you tomorrow," promised Caiti. Tom gave her a quick kiss and at last we were away.

Laying my head back on the head rest I watched the sun flickering through the trees, and thought back over the events of the day. What a lovely family the Fullertons were I mused. Paul, the younger brother, we had not met because he had gone to Wymondham to buy a part for a tractor. A very subdued Caiti sat in the back of the car waving for as long as Tom was visible, then she gave a sigh and settled back.

"This must be Primrose Lane," stated Jim, as a right hand turn loomed ahead. I peered out of the window and saw a finger post almost covered over by a wild rose hedge.

"Yes, it is," I informed him. Jim turned into the lane and we continued on our way.

And then it happened! One moment we were driving in brilliant sunshine then suddenly we were in the thickest fog I have ever experienced. The road ahead was totally obliterated and Jim was straining his eyes to see the roadside verges. Then calamity! The car gave a sudden judder and stopped completely.

"Oh dear, what's wrong with it?" I asked.

"Goodness only knows," Jim answered sharply. "It can't be out of petrol. I'll see if I can push it off the road in case some other car comes along."

Caiti and I got out to help and between us we pushed the car almost into a hedge. Jim fumbled about in the car boot until he found a torch which we kept there in case of emergencies. Pulling up the bonnet he shone the light around while Caiti and I stood and shivered in our light summer dresses.

"I know I'm not the best mechanic in the land," Jim announced, "but there doesn't seem to be anything wrong."

"My mobile is in the door pocket," I remembered. "Shall we ring Tom and ask him to get some help to us?"

Jim retrieved the phone from the car and started to tap in the number Caiti gave him. Nothing happened.

"Bother," I said "it must be the battery."

"No," Jim said. "It was on the charger until we set out this morning. Probably the signal can't get through this fog. I've never known anything as thick as this." Jim shone the light around and then we could just make out a large iron gateway, quite close to where we were standing.

"Good," he said. "There must be a house down there, perhaps they will let us use their phone."

"I'm c-cold," wailed Caiti. Remembering there was a rug in the boot of the car, I quickly pulled it out and Caiti and I wrapped it around our shoulders. Jim locked up the car and the three of us began to walk along the drive towards a very large house which was just becoming visible through the fog.

"Can you smell smoke?" I asked.

"Probably someone with a bonfire," Jim replied.

At last we reached the front of the house. We could just make out the position of the front door and with the aid of Jim's torch, found the knocker which was shaped like some strange animal. Jim knocked loudly on the door. We could see no chinks anywhere in any of the many windows and no-one came to answer the door.

"Try again," I told him. "Perhaps they are in the back of the house, or maybe they have gone out for the day."

Caiti groaned. "I hope not," she said, "I'm really cold."

Jim lifted the knocker and gave the door a hefty rat-a-tat-tat. We waited, but no-one appeared. Locating the door knob I turned it and to our amazement the door opened. Succumbing to my curiosity I stepped inside, quickly followed by Caiti.

"We can't just walk in," protested Jim, but following us all the same.

"Hello," I shouted. "Is anyone at home?" There was no reply. Jim shone his torch around and we found we were standing in a large hallway with doors going off to the left and right and a wide staircase to the rear. The staircase divided at the top, landings going off to the left and right but it was too dark to see it all properly. Caiti opened the first door on the right and peeped in.

"Oh look," she said, "there's a lovely log fire. I'm going to get warm."

Jim was shining the torch up and down the walls by the front door.

"What are you doing?" I asked him.

"Looking for a light switch."

"Of course, I hadn't thought of that."

"There doesn't seem to be one."

"Don't be silly, there must be."

Jim moved the torch light upwards and there in the centre of the ceiling was a large candelabra.

"See," I said. "They've got to turn that on somewhere."

Jim laughed. "Have another look."

I did, and then noticed what Jim had already seen.

"Candles," I exclaimed.

"Yes, and more in sconces on the walls," he commented.

"Very strange," I remarked. "Perhaps the electricity doesn't come this far out."

"A house this size would have its own generator or something if that were the case."

I agreed and puzzled we went to find Caiti. She was curled up on a rug in front of the fire, almost asleep. The large fire gave out quite a good light and we looked around us with interest.

The room was furnished very sparsely but what furniture there was was extremely old. There was one box-seated, heavy framed armchair, several ornately carved stools, two settles and a black japanned cabinet on a gilt base. Over in the corner stood a harpsichord. Although the overall impression of the room was hard and comfortless, it was softened somewhat with coloured cushions and woollen shawls. Persian rugs were scattered about the wooden floor. Jim, who knew quite a bit about antiques, was fascinated by it all.

"Whatever possessed them to furnish the room like this," I wondered.

"It looks as if they have furnished it in keeping with the age of the house," Jim observed. "These things are worth thousands and they went out and left the door unlocked! I'll light a few of these candles, then we can have an even better look." Taking a taper from a silver box in the hearth, he lit the candles that were placed around. Suddenly I heard a sound!

"Shush," I whispered. "W-What's that?" Jim froze where he stood and Caiti sat up.

Footsteps slow and heavy were coming towards the door to our sanctuary. I quickly ran to Jim and grabbed his arm. Although the fire gave out an amazing heat I turned quite cold. The door knob turned and the door opened to reveal an elderly woman carrying a tray. This she placed on a stool beside Caiti, who was now wide awake.

"Your favourites," the woman said, and after putting another log on the fire she left the room, without even glancing in our direction. Jim suddenly came to life and rushed to the door.

"I say," he called, "have you a phone we can use?" The woman had disappeared.

'A servant I expect,' I thought. She had been dressed in a long black gown, almost covered by a white pinafore and had worn a lace cap.

"Oh well," said Jim, "perhaps she'll come back. Let's see what she's brought us."

The tray contained a dish of pasties, a plate of cinnamon cakes, a small straight-sided teapot with a conical lid and three pewter handleless dishes which we presumed to be tea cups. There was also a little dish of honey but no milk.

"I could do with a cup of tea," Jim remarked, "but I've never tried it without milk though."

"Put a little honey in it," instructed Caiti. "You'll find it has a lovely flavour."

Although we'd eaten quite a large lunch, I was feeling quite peckish and picked up one of the pasties. The pastry was delicious and the meat inside quite heavenly. I asked Caiti what the meat was and she told me 'pheasant'. It wasn't until I'd half eaten my pasty that something odd struck me.

"Caiti," I queried, "what did that woman mean when she said that these were your favourites? How come she knew what you like to eat?" Caiti gave me one of her 'Mona Lisa' smiles and nibbling on her pasties she stared dreamily into the fire. "Don't try and tell me you've been here before," I told her.

"This was not a happy house," was all the answer she gave.

Noticing that her eyes now had the same glazed look that I had seen at the farm, I made a mental note to take her to my doctor as soon as we arrived home. We made short work of the pasties and the cakes and the tea was very refreshing.

Soon Jim got to his feet and once more paced about the room, studying the pictures on the walls. Caiti joined him and when they reached the harpsichord she pulled up a stool and commenced to play 'Greensleeves'.

"I didn't know you could play," I remarked. Caiti laughed. "Oh, Aunt Rose insisted on me learning all the ladylike pursuits. Music, ballet, needlework and then art, which I loved. So although I lived on a sheep station and rode a horse most of the time I was out of school, I do know a lot about gentler activities."

"You are a complete enigma," I told her smiling. "We learn something new about you every day."

We spent a pleasant evening listening to Caiti play and we sang whenever we knew the songs. The uneasiness I had been feeling ever since we had entered this strange house was beginning to fade – but then the hairs on the back of my neck rose as footsteps again sounded outside the door. We stood there in a group around the harpsichord as the door opened and the old servant again entered, this time carrying a lighted candle in a wooden candlestick holder.

"Your rooms are prepared, "she said, in a dry, harsh voice. "Please follow me."

I looked at Jim and he must have seen the fright in my eyes.

"Excuse me, but exactly what sort of place is this?" he asked.

Before he could ask more the old woman patted her ear and beckoned us to go with her.

"That's all we need," Jim muttered. "She's deaf! Come on we'd better see where she's taking us."

Trembling I took his hand and with Caiti following we went out into the hall and were then led up the staircase, along a landing and into a room which held a massive four poster bed. The woman placed the candlestick on a chest of drawers, and then crossed over to open the door of an adjoining room.

"For you Miss Kate," she said and disappeared into the darkness of the other room. "I will light your candle." We saw a flicker of light appear, then a door closed and she was gone.

"That woman frightens me," I admitted. "There's something about her that makes my flesh creep." Jim agreed the whole experience was weird.

"I am wondering if this is some sort of theme park," he said. "You know, like the ones that stage 'Who done it?' weekends. It would explain why she seemed to expect us."

"You mean that probably a party of three had booked, and, when we turned up she took them for us?"

"That's right. So come on, let's try out this bed. It looks comfortable enough."

"I could do with a loo and a good wash," I said. "Do you think that door leads to a bathroom?" I had noticed a door to the left of the bed.

"Try it."

I did, after lighting another candle, and found myself in a small room containing a wash stand on which stood a bowl and ewer of hot water. On opening a door in the washstand I discovered a chamber pot! 'Luxury indeed!' I thought. Jim followed me in and after a swift freshen up, we went to see what Caiti was doing. Her room, though smaller, contained a four poster bed and also a washstand which was equipped much the same as ours. She was drying her face with a rough towel.

"Lock that door Jim," I ordered, "I don't feel safe."

"What about nightwear?" Jim asked.

Caiti pointed to a white voluminous gown which hung over a chair beside the bed. On investigation, Jim and I found similar ones complete with mob cap for me and a long tasselled one for him. After we'd all had a good giggle, we decided to sleep in our underwear. Locking our door and leaving the one into Caiti's room wide open, we climbed into bed. Jim leaned over and blew out the candle.

"Can't we leave it alight?" I asked. "This house is so creepy."

"Better not," Jim replied. "The candle may fall over or something. I don't fancy being burned."

"Jim!" I exclaimed, shuddering at the thought. "Come here silly," Jim laughed and pulled me into his arms. "You're quite safe with me."

I did not expect to sleep a wink but must have quickly dozed off to spend a long dreamless sleep. When I awoke my watch said it was seven thirty. Turning I went to wake Jim but found his side of the bed was empty. My nervousness returned and I rapidly climbed out of the enormous bed, pulled my dress quickly over my head and padded across to Caiti's room. It was empty! I panicked and ran across to the door and out on to the landing. Caiti was there studying the pictures along the corridor. Of Jim there was no sign.

"Oh Caiti," I cried, "I thought you had deserted me."

"Don't be silly," she smiled. "You were in such a deep sleep we thought it best not to wake you."

"Where is Jim then?"

"He said he was going to explore since the fog is a lot thinner now."

I glanced towards a window.

"So it is," I said. "As soon as Jim comes back I think we'd better be going, don't you?"

Caiti agreed and I joined her to study the pictures. Most of them were portraits but here and there was a landscape. Caiti stopped by one of these and turning to me said, "You know I'm positive we've seen this picture before. Wasn't it on the wall of Tom's inn?"

After careful scrutiny I agreed. "Tom's must be a copy. Either that or the artist painted two."

Caiti walked further along the corridor and I found myself at the head of the staircase. There on the wall hung a large portrait of a beautiful young girl. She was wearing a blue gown and her golden hair hung like a shawl around her shoulders. I looked at the face and my heart missed a beat. Green eyes looked into mine and I felt myself becoming mesmerised. Dragging my eyes away I called for Caiti.

"What is it?" she asked, joining me.

"Look," I gasped. "The portrait! It's you!" Caiti looked up. Green eyes met green eyes. Caiti collapsed at my feet in a dead faint.

Part Two
1646

Kate Ashe sat at the window of her attic room gazing dreamily at the rustic view before her, the embroidery she had been doing lying forgotten on her lap. The room had once been her nursery and was now her refuge and hide-away when day to day problems proved too much for her. Here she could relax, play her lute, do her embroidery or, as now, just gaze out of the window. In the distance the river meandered through meadows dotted with sheep until it disappeared into the wood and out of view. Nearer home brown and white cattle ambled along chewing the lush green grass and Kate could hear the soft lowing sound they made intermingled with wonderful bird song. Down in the yard she could see the servants going about their allotted tasks, laughing and joking as they did so. A gentle sigh escaped from Kate's soft lips.

"A silver farthing for your thoughts Miss Kate." Kate jumped and turned to find her one time nurse had entered the room.

"Oh Nella! you startled me," she cried. "I failed to hear the door open."

Eleanor Masters laughed. "I noticed," she said. "But why the big sigh?"

Kate turned her face to the window again.

"Just look at the view Nella. Is it not so very peaceful? Yet the whole country is at war. Terrible deeds are being done. Villages have been destroyed, men taken away from their homes to fight for a cause they know naught about, many will never return. Oh Nella, I fear for my dear father and pray that he will be safe."

As a small child Kate had been unable to master the name Eleanor, much to her mother's disgust. Paul, Kate's brother, could enunciate all words perfectly as soon as he could speak. 'Nella' was as near as Kate could manage and the name had stuck.

"Try not to fear, my dear one," Nella instructed now. "It is quite likely that your father, Sir Denzil, is in France on one of his Highness King Charles' missions."

"I do hope so," replied Kate.

Sir Denzil was one of the King's most loyal supporters and greatest friends. Serving as an emissary he was frequently abroad for long periods and often in great danger both in France and England. On the rare occasions when he was able to get home to Marley, he brought with him wonderful items for his household; beautiful silver and fabrics from France, rugs from Persia and porcelain from China and Holland. Quite a few good pieces of silverware had been stolen when the Parliamentarians swept through Norfolk three years earlier. Hardly any Royalist homes were left unscathed as Cromwell's army searched out Royalists and Papists who refused to join the Parliamentary cause. Many gentlemen may have been genuine neutrals but Cromwell fearing the Papists in Norfolk were going to rise against him had had them all arrested.

Roundheads had searched Marley Manor from attic to cellar but Sir Denzil was away. Angrily the soldiers stole many valuables and seized all the best horses from the stables. The last three years had been fairly peaceful except for the odd skirmish round and about.

Kate shook her lovely blonde hair back from her face and looked at Nella with amazing green eyes.

"Is it time for my portrait sitting?" she asked.

Nella nodded. "I have your gown ready, if you will come to your room Miss Kate."

Together they descended the stairs to Kate's suite of rooms on the first floor.

"I have a message from your mother, Lady Maria," stated Nella as she helped Kate into a simple silk gown. A beautiful shade of blue, the gown was cut away at the front to show an underskirt of white Flemish lace and had full padded sleeves of blue silk trimmed with matching lace.

"You look a picture," breathed Nella, brushing Kate's unruly hair into submission.

"So what does my lady mother demand?" asked Kate.

"She wishes you to attend her the moment your sitting is over."

Kate groaned. "Have you any notion as to why?"

Nella shook her head. "No dearest, but I do know that she is expecting Lord Monksleigh to call this afternoon."

"Oh no, if only Father would come home! It is now common knowledge hereabouts that he is being cuckolded by that oaf of a man."

"Hush dear," Nella warned. "We do not know for certain but I admit it does seem likely. Now run along to your sitting and try to keep calm."

Just over an hour later Kate entered her mother's retiring room. Lady Maria was seated on an ornately carved chair, her gown of pale pink silk spread around her. The over-dress was of a deeper shade of pink decorated with red velvet bows. The sleeves were slashed to show the padded under sleeves and a red stomacher flattened her ample bosom – so tightly had it been fastened. Her hair, now a greying brown, was brushed back from her face and caught up on top of her head with a jewelled headdress.

"Rather overdressed for an afternoon," thought Kate as she walked over to her mother.

For a few seconds Lady Maria did not notice her daughter as she was laughing up into the face of the man standing by her, a tall thin man with a pointed black beard. Kate had time to take in his manner of dress before her mother turned. His brown velvet doublet and his hose were exceedingly shabby, the cream cossack of watered silk trimmed with lace was at least twenty years out of date.

"Ah, there you are Katherine," said Lady Maria. "Come and meet Lord Monksleigh."

Kate executed a swift curtsey.

"Charmed to meet you again m'dear," said his Lordship holding out his hand.

Kate touched her fingers to his then hastily drew her hand away. Even that small contact filled her with revulsion.

"We have a surprise for you Katherine," announced Lady Maria. "Lord Monksleigh has brought his son along to meet you. I am sure you will get along together very well."

A young man rose from a seat in the window recess and came slowly towards them. Fate had not been kind to Colin Monksleigh. His dark hair hung long and lank, his nose was over long and his teeth were slightly prominent. He was suffering badly from teenage spots. Kate's first reaction to him was one of pity, so she smiled as he bowed to her. Before Colin could speak Lord Monksleigh came forward and placing an arm around them steered them to the door.

"Now go out into the garden and get to know each other," he said. "Do not forget my advice Colin. Lady Maria and I will have a game of cards in your absence," he added with a salacious grin and Maria tittered in the background.

Alone in the hall, the young couple looked at each other shyly. Colin looked very ill at ease and fiddled with the lacy cuffs on the short velvet coat that he wore.

"Please wait here," Kate said. "I must change my gown and shoes. I will not be many moments."

Colin nodded and Kate fled upstairs to her room. Nella was sitting sewing a petticoat when Kate burst into the room.

"Quick Nella," she said, "help me out of this gown and find me something less flimsy. I have to show Colin Monksleigh around the garden. Heaven knows what topics we shall find to discuss. He looks such a lack lustre boy."

Nella frowned. "Trust not in looks, Kate. If he takes after his father then no young woman is safe in his company."

Kate laughed. "He looks harmless enough – but just in case I will arm myself."

So saying she took a long bodkin from her etui and secreted it in her fan. Once outside Kate led the way along a path and down three steps which led into a parterre garden, neatly trimmed and weed free.

"I expect you have much grander gardens at Monksleigh," Kate said, glancing sideways at Colin who was walking silently beside her.

"Oh, n-no," he stuttered, "Father has let most of the gardeners go."

"To join the King or Cromwell you mean?"

A dull red flush crept up Colin's neck and face. He stared at the path as he admitted,   "No Miss Ashe. Father could not afford to pay them."

Kate's eyes widened in horror. "What happened to them then? They must have had families! Did your father let them stay in their cottages?"

Colin looked even more crestfallen. "With no work they could not pay the rent so Father had them turned out. A few of the younger men obtained work on other farms so they were able to stay."

"And what about the old and infirm?" demanded Kate. "What happened to them?"

Colin shook his head. "I know not, Miss Ashe. I pleaded with Father to let them stay but he was adamant, and so they packed up their few belongings and left."

By now the young couple had reached a hedge and passing through an archway they entered a rose garden, sheltered all around by tall brick walls. Wooden benches were placed here and there and Kate sat down on one of these and motioned Colin to sit beside her. Nervously he did so.

Boiling with anger Kate faced Colin as she said, "I have never had any liking for your father, Colin, and now I like him even less. My father does not treat his servants so cruelly. What kind of man is he that treats human beings worse than cattle?"

Colin stared down at his feet, his head bowed and his hands

clenching and unclenching. Kate, noticing his discomfiture, placed her hand gently on his.

"I am so sorry Colin. I should not have criticised your father so. Please forgive me."

Colin jumped to his feet. "You have every right Miss Ashe to speak your mind, but I beg you do not think that I would behave so unseemly."

Kate smiled and rose from her seat. "Come," she said, "let us not be melancholy on such a beautiful day. Do not the roses smell delightful and are they not beautiful?"

"Not nearly as beautiful as you, Miss Ashe," he replied shyly.

"Why Colin," Kate laughed, "where have you learnt such pretty speech? Oh, and if we are to be friends you will please call me Kate, Katherine is such a bore."

Colin's pale face lit up. "I would like very much to be your friend." Then, shamefacedly he added, "other than my sisters I have never spoken to any other young ladies."

"Goodness," Kate cried, "where have you been hiding? But come let us continue our walk whilst you tell me all about yourself."

Slowly they began to walk again along the paths between the rose beds.

"Well come along Colin – I'm waiting."

"My life is not worth the telling," he replied.

"I shall be the judge of that," Kate stated smiling. "Now how old are you?"

"I am in my eighteenth year."

"And I in my seventeenth year. Now go on from there. Where were you educated for instance?"

Colin began. "I was very ill as a young child. It started with measles but after that I suffered many complaints mainly to do with my chest and Father was tired of me being so weak. My mother could not give me much of her time as she already had two more babies to tend so Father decided to pack me off to some distant relations in Suffolk." Colin paused, looking distressed, and then went on. "I hated it there. The tutor was a cruel man and he beat us boys mercilessly if we could not learn our Latin. He especially picked on me, and the three brothers of the family thought it amusing to follow his lead."

Kate, looking shocked, broke in. "How old were you then Colin?"

"Four years," he answered. "They were supposed to teach me to duel with swords and other such things but the swords they gave me I could not hold because I was so weak. The other boys laughed when I cried. When I was five years old I ran away, but of course they caught me and the tutor beat me near to death. I was locked in a room until my father came to collect me."

Kate looked aghast. "What a terrible story!" she said. "What happened next? Did you remain at home?"

Colin shook his head. "No, Father took me to an abbey and put me into the care of the monks there. The abbey had been badly damaged years before during the Dissolution, but the brothers were kind to me and I was happy there and although there was very little to eat they shared all they had with me. My mother died when I was six years old."

"So how long have you been back at home?" Kate asked, compassion showing in her green eyes.

"About six months I suppose," Colin answered. "Father realised I was old enough to take over some of the responsibilities for the estate and-and-," he stammered to a halt, his face reddening again. Colin hesitated for some moments, his pale face working as if he were trying to force the words out. Then he spoke in a rush.

"Father wishes me to marry because a bride's dowry would help pay off some of his debts."

Kate stared at him, then suddenly she smiled and the smile turned to a laugh.

"I am beginning to understand," she giggled, trying to hide behind her fan. "I am supposed to be the blushing bride!"

Colin hung his head and could not answer.

"And do you wish to marry?" she asked.

He shook his head miserably.

"Good," she replied, "neither do I – at least not yet for a few years."

"Please do not laugh," Colin explained, "but I would like to become a priest."

"I am sure you would make a fine priest."

Colin gave Kate a weak smile. "But I am the eldest son, so therefore the heir to the title and the estate. Benjamin, my younger brother, is far stronger and able than I. Willingly I would give it all to him, but Father will not hear of it."

"Hmm," mused Kate, "there must be a way out but at the moment I cannot think of one."

Silently they walked on, leaving the garden and entering the courtyard, where chickens busily scratching in the earth, scuttled out of the way clucking noisily as they did so. Abruptly Kate halted, and turning to Colin said, "I have thought of a great idea Colin. If your father and my mother wish to marry us off then let them think their plan is working. It is too soon today but in a week or so we will announce our betrothal. Are you good at play acting? Could you pretend to have a liking for me?"

Colin flushed with pleasure. "Oh, I do have a liking for you Kate. You are very kind and if I wished to wed I am sure there is no one better."

"Good," Kate said. "When we are near to our respective parents we will act like a couple of turtle doves. You must kiss my hand at every opportunity and I will flutter my eyelashes at you over my fan. Now come, I will introduce you to Cook."

Giggling together like a couple of children, they crossed the yard and entered the kitchen.

Betsy Kirk, a plump, jolly, red-faced woman, was up to her elbows in flour. Seeing Kate she jumped, scattering flour all over herself and the floor.

"Mistress Kate," she cried, bobbing a floury curtsey. "Wut iver do yer mean a comin in the back way? You fair med me jump. I thought as'ow it were one o' the mawthers."

"Sorry Cook," replied Kate, "Colin and I were looking

around the gardens and I suddenly thought I would bring him to see you. Colin, come and meet Betsy, our cook. Betsy, this is Sir Colin – son of Lord Monksleigh."

Colin, not quite knowing what to do started to put out his hand, then changed his mind and bowed instead.

"Forgive me," he said, "but I have never been into our kitchens and have no idea of the etiquette required."

Betsy gave him a curtsey then went on mixing the flour and water in a bowl, saying as she did so, "Mistress Kate's mother would be roight roiled if she knew you war 'ere. Staff and gentry dunt mix."

Kate pulled a face. "Fiddlesticks," she retorted. "I enjoy coming here."

Colin was watching Betsy with interest as she took a handful of dough and formed it into a ball placing it down on a platter.

"What are you making?" he asked.

Betsy smiled. "Norfolk dumlins," she answered. "Or we call 'em Norfolk Swimmers. Thass onla flar an' water an' a little bitta salt. Then yer mix it up an' pop 'em inta the stew fer exactly twenty minutes, but yer dissent tairke the lid orf cus if yer do they tan inter cannon balls."

During all this exchange, a small girl was quietly stirring a cauldron hanging from a spit over the open fire. A most mouth-watering smell wafted across the kitchen.

Colin peered in.

"This smells good Cook. I suppose it is for the dining room tonight."

"Lawks no," laughed Betsy. "Tis only rabbit stew. This is for the staff. Wud yer loike a taste?"

Colin nodded and Betsy instructed the young kitchen maid to fetch a bowl and some bread and to lay a place at the large kitchen table. Cook filled the bowl to the brim and put it before Colin, saying, "Forgive me young sir but yer looks loike yer cud do with feedin' up. Dunt they feed yer uvver at the hall?"

"Not like this they don't," he replied, giving Betsy a grateful smile.

Betsy looked into the cauldron to make sure that it was boiling and then dropped in the dumplings and quickly put on the lid. "That's that," she remarked. "Now we must set the table 'afore the 'ungry wuns appear."

Kate noticed that Colin had cleared up the very last spoonful of his stew and so, thanking Betsy, she motioned for Colin to follow her. He did so after thanking Betsy most profusely and bowing to her once more. Kate led him through a door at the back of the kitchen which opened onto the back passage and then up some stairs leading to Lady Maria's suite.

"I-I hope I did right bowing to your cook," Colin stammered. "At home we are taught to ignore our servants. In fact, if one is seen in any of our rooms or corridors they are immediately dismissed."

"How are they supposed to clean the rooms then?" Kate demanded.

"They have to rise at five of the clock and get ready the rooms used by the family. Only the housekeeper and the footmen, oh, and the parlour maid are allowed to be seen during the day."

Kate's green eyes flashed. "How I wish I could be mistress there for a while. There would be some big alterations. Servants are human beings too, and I know Betsy was extremely proud that you bowed to her, even if it was not the correct etiquette. In future a nod of the head will suffice."

Colin smiled. "I have much to learn," he said.

"I shall take you in hand," Kate laughed. "First we will do something about those spots. Can you meet me tomorrow at noon by the mill?"

"Of course," Colin agreed, "be pleased to."

By now they had reached the door to Lady Maria's retiring room and after exchanging a conspiratorial grin they entered the room.

* * * * *

The next morning Kate awoke early. Dawn was only just

breaking and sitting halfway up in bed, she looked at the clock hanging on her wall. Four thirty it read! Kate groaned and lay back on her pillow and attempted to get back to sleep. Sleep eluded her and after tossing and turning for what seemed ages she gave in and sat up.

Somewhere a blackbird started to sing and then others joined in – thrushes, sparrows, doves, until every bird in the neighbourhood was united in a wonderful cacophony of sound. Kate sat entranced until as gradually as it had started it began to fade away. Slowly the sky began to lighten and the new day had begun.

Slipping from her bed, Kate quickly pulled on the clothes which Nella had left ready. Locating a woollen shawl from her dressing chest and slipping her feet into soft kid slippers, she left her bed-chamber and quietly ran up the back stairs to the servants' quarters and so into her private room. Sitting by the window Kate let her thoughts dwell on the happenings of the previous day.

"I wonder if Colin is awake?" she thought. "What a gentle, thoughtful lad he is – but so unhappy. Somehow I am going to change all that."

Sighing Kate picked up a crayon and began to sketch the view from the window. It was then that she heard a commotion coming from one of the servants' rooms further along the corridor. Putting down her sketch pad Kate went out to investigate and was just in time to see a servant girl running down the back stairs. The sound of sobbing reached Kate's ears and she hurried along the corridor until she found the room from whence it came. Pushing open the door Kate saw a very young girl kneeling on the floor trying to mop up a pool of water. Two frightened eyes looked up at Kate as she entered.

"Why, whatever has happened?" Kate enquired, "don't cry dear, it will all dry up soon. Did you have an accident?"

The young servant nodded, still sniffing and wringing out the floor cloth.

"It's my bed Miss," she explained in a wobbly voice. "It's soaking wet. I shall git suffin rong when Cook finds out, an-an it'll never be dry fer ternight." Tears streamed down her face again.

Kate glanced at the livery bed. It consisted of no more than a straw filled mattress on a wooden pallet, covered with a rough cotton spread. The straw mattress was dripping water on to the floor. Kate was appalled and anger brought red patches to her cheeks as she thought of the opulence of her own bed-chamber and the poor state of this room. The only furniture in the room was a wooden chest on which was placed a cracked basin and jug and a smaller box under the window. Seeing that the girl had almost stopped crying, Kate took her arms and gently lifted her to her feet.

"Now tell me what happened," she said, "I have a feeling that it has something to do with the girl I saw racing down the stairs. Am I correct?"

"Y-yes Miss. Cook sent me to scrub the corridor and w-when I got here she was looking through my box and when I said as how they wuz my private things she pushed me and the bucket o'water went evra where." Tears flowed once more.

Kate hugged the girl to her. 'She's no more than a child,' she thought.

"What is your given name?" she asked.

"B-Betty, Miss."

"Well, Betty, we will sort this mess out. Can you help me with the mattress?"

Betty looked shocked. "Miss you mussn't lift that. Thass servants' work."

"Tosh," replied Kate. "Just lift that end and between us we will push it down the stairs. Firstly, though, you had better hang the coverlet on the window sill. It will soon dry there."

Together they heaved the sodden mattress along the corridor and pushed it down the back stairs until it came to rest on the landing below.

"We'll leave it there for now," Kate said, wiping her wet hands on her gown. "Now come back to your room, I wish to see what can be done to make the room more comfortable."

There were four rooms before the one in which Betty slept. Kate opened each door and peered in. All were practically bare save for the livery beds and dilapidated wash stands. Back in Betty's room Kate looked around in disgust. The walls were bare and needed white-washing. She looked at the little box which contained the few clothes Betty owned.

"Is this what the other servant was looking in?" Kate asked.

Betty nodded. "She musta bin lookin' for my little bird."

"Your bird?"

"Yis Miss, let me show yer."

Betty dived into her meagre belongings and soon proudly held up a wooden bird for Kate's inspection.

"Why that is exquisite," Kate exclaimed. "How did you come by it?"

Betty stroked the wooden feathers.

"Me uncle whittled it for me."

"He must be very clever, it is so life like."

"It's all he can do, Miss, yer see he wuz borned all 'rong."

"What do you mean Betty?" Kate asked.

"Well Mam sez 'is 'ead wuz too big and he took too long to be borned and 'is mam died."

Kate's eyes filled with tears and she felt a lump in her throat. It was with great difficulty that she now asked, "And does he live in the village?"

"Yis Miss, wi' me Granma and Grandad."

"Then I will visit him this morning and ask him to carve me a bird, for which I shall pay him handsomely – but now what are we going to do about you? Would you like to move into another room on the other side of the corridor?"

Kate was surprised to see tears sparkling in Betty's eyes and her lips trembled as she said "Oh no Miss, oi love this room," and pointing out of the small attic room window she added, "yer see Miss I can see the windmill from here. Thass me home cus Dad's the miller and oi fill close so long as oi kin see it. Dad sez 'e'll put a lamp in the top winder when it gits dark so's I know they're still there an oi kin see the loight if oi weark up in the noight."

Kate caught the little girl and hugged her tight to her chest.

"Do not fret," she told her, "you shall keep your room, but for tonight you will sleep in my room further along the corridor and you will still see the mill. I shall get some of the menservants up here with whitewash to brighten the walls, so take up your box and bring it to my room."

Betty followed Kate along the corridor hugging her meagre belongings to her thin chest. Opening her door Kate stood aside to allow Betty to enter. The child's face was a picture as she looked around at the furniture and decorations.

"Ooo Miss," she breathed, "it's bootiful. Oi kin sleep in the chair at the foot o'yer bed."

Kate laughed. "That's only a day bed," she exclaimed. "My bed chamber is on the floor below. I use this room to hide away in if I feel a need to be alone. So tonight you shall sleep in a feather bed."

Betty's eyes shone. "Oh, Miss," was all she could say.

"Now we must go downstairs and have words with Nella and Cook."

So saying Kate led the way down the two flights of stairs and into the kitchen, where they found Nella giving Cook the menu for the day's meals. Quickly explaining what had happened and what she intended to do, Kate was about to leave when the sight of a young boy lounging outside by the wall made her go to the open door and call.

"You boy. Come at once we need your help."

The boy shuffled shamefaced to the door, head hanging low.

"Oi wer only hevvin a rest Miss. Thass heavy wark a haulin' them pairls up."

"Just you watch your mouth young Jed," Cook interjected, "oi yer'll foind yerself heddin hummuds."

Jed raised his head, and Kate was thunderstruck to see the fright in the boy's brown eyes.

"It is alright, Jed," she said. "I just want you to help Betty bring down her mattress and put it out in the sun, and then mayhap you can find some white-wash and paint her bedroom walls. Can you do that?"

Jed nodded, relief showing in his face and in the way his wiry young body relaxed.

"Yis Miss," he said. "Moi dad shew me how ter do it afore he got kilt in the war." Tears filled his eyes.

"So now you are the man of the house?" Kate questioned.

"Yis Miss."

"And how old are you Jed?"

"Ten Miss."

"Do you have other brothers and sisters?"

"Four sisters and wun brother, Miss, but oim the eldest," he added.

Kate looked at the boy's thin body and at his threadbare clothes and noticed he was barefooted. Making a mental note to do something about this family she smiled gently and sent him with Betty to retrieve her mattress.

"I shall be breaking my fast with my mother today," Kate announced, anger showing in her eyes and the pinkness of her face. "Things are going to be a lot different around here from now on. If Mi-lady will not bother herself with our servants' welfare then I will, and I shall enjoy telling her so."

So saying she opened the door that led from the kitchen into the back hallway and disappeared through it, leaving Nella and Cook with a mixture of astonishment and amusement on their faces.

It was mid-morning when Kate set forth upon her visit to Marley village. Sitting high upon her favourite horse she was able to relax at last and enjoy the ride. Breakfast with her mother had been anything but a happy occasion. Sharp words had issued from one side of the table to the other. Lady Maria stated that the servants' quarters were none of her business and that Nella was supposed to be in charge of the housekeeping. Kate had snapped back that without cash Nella was unable to improve the servants' lot. Lady Maria had indignantly asked what the housekeeping money was spent on and was informed that three quarters of it went on new furniture and other luxuries for Lady Maria's suite of rooms. The other quarter barely covered food and wages. Kate knew that Nella went without her wages quite often so that Cook was able to buy the necessities she needed to keep a good table. Lady Maria then stated that they must get rid of some of the staff. A furious Kate then hit out that the first to go should be Maria's personal maid since she did nothing all day but dress her mistress and play cards until summoned to do some other trivial task. A purple faced Lady Maria had ordered Kate to leave her presence at once and Kate still quivering with anger had done so.

Now her anger abated Kate looked about her. The rough country road was bordered by hedges and trees. The hedges were interwoven with the pale pink of wild roses and the yellow of honeysuckle. Tall foxgloves and scarlet poppies adorned the roadside. Except for the gentle clip clop of the horse's hooves, it was quiet enough to hear the buzz of the bees as they vied with colourful butterflies to be the first to sip nectar from one of the many flowers. Kate smiled as a baby rabbit ran into the road, saw the horse and then quickly sped back into the undergrowth. Soon the road divided and Kate turned her horse to the left. A few yards further on the village lay before her.

Marley was not a large village but possessed a round towered church with a thatched nave attached. The priest's house stood next to it but set back a bit from the road. Passing church and house Kate drew her horse to a halt and glanced around her. The large village green was a hive of activity and most of the occupants of the dozen or so cottages seemed to be engaged in some kind of decorating or booth building. Suddenly, a rose-faced middle aged woman came running across the grass towards Kate, crying out as she did so.

"Miss Kate, Mistress Kate, how good to see yer. It must be months since yer come ter the village."

Kate laughed. "It's good to see you too Agnes, I need some of your salves to help a friend of mine – but what is happening on the green?"

"Thass Midsummer's Day termorrer and we're getting ready fer the fair," Agnes explained. "Thass allus good fun. Hent you eva bin?"

Shaking her head, Kate got down from her horse.

"No" she answered, "not that I can remember but I will make sure that the servants from the Manor get time off to come. Now, Agnes, I must not delay you so if you could get the salve I need I will be on my way."

Agnes led Kate to one of the cottages and bade her tie the horse to an oak tree nearby.

"Would yer care ter step inside?" she asked hesitantly as she held open the door. "It's not much but it's clean."

Kate entered the small room which was sparsely furnished with just a table and three odd wooden chairs. An earthenware pot holding a few golden marigolds stood on the windowsill giving a homely touch to the room. Agnes indicated one of the chairs and after giving it a quick flick with her voluminous sackcloth apron, she invited her guest to sit.

"Now then Miss Kate," she said, "which one of my salves wid yer be needin'?"

"Something to get rid of spots and boils," Kate replied, "oh yes, do you have anything to improve his hair? It is so greasy and lank."

Agnes chuckled. "I hev just what he needs," she said. "If you will excuse me whoile I pop into the back room."

So saying and not waiting for an answer she disappeared through the inner door and Kate could hear her sorting among her various pots. Eventually she emerged carrying three pots, two flatish ones and one taller one which sounded as if it contained liquid.

"Here yer are me dear. These should do the trick." Agnes placed the pots on the table near to Kate. "This one is for spots," she explained. "It's a mixture of bergamot, sweet thyme, chamomile, juniper and lavender. Tell him to rub a little on his face twice a day an' he'll soon see the difference. The liquid in this pot is to close up the pores of the skin wunce the salve has done it's work. It's only my recipe med mainly from witch hazel. This 'ere pot is fer 'is hair an' it's med up with juniper, rosemary and camomile. If he's unlucky enough to git a push on his neck then tell him to pick a bunch of chickweed outer the garden, simmer it to a pulp with verra little water and put it on the push while it's still hot."

"Goodness," Kate laughed. "Poor Colin. But I am sure he will be pleased with the results. Now let me pay you Agnes. How much do I owe you?"

"Mistress Kate!" Agnes cried, "I cannot take your money. 'Tis a pleasure to help yoi."

"Tosh," replied Kate, "you cannot live on fresh air. You will take this with grateful thanks."

So saying she pressed a silver crown into Agnes' hand and carefully picking up her purchases she rose from the chair and walked to the door. Agnes had tears in her eyes as she followed Kate out into the sunshine. For a while they stood together watching all the bustle on the green, then Kate unhitched her horse and turned to Agnes.

"Where will I find a man who carves birds and animals and has a niece who works at the Manor?" she asked.

"You must mean Freddie," Agnes said, "he lives over the green in the cottage by the inn, you will see……….."

Her voice trailed away as she realised Kate was not listening but was staring wide-eyed and open-mouthed at a young man riding a bay-coloured mare pulling a tumbrel of hay.

"Who is that young man?" Kate asked when her heart had stopped thumping and her breath returned to normal.

Agnes laughed. "That's young Tom Fullerton," she explained. "His father has the farm on Mill Road but young Tom has to do most of the work cus old Tom lost a leg when he wuz fighting with Cromwell's lot at Marston Moor."

"That hair," Kate breathed, "I have never seen such a beautiful colour. It's neither red nor gold."

"Takes after his mother," Agnes volunteered. "By the look of him he can't tearke his eyes off you either."

Kate blushed deep pink, then stowing the pots into her saddlebag she put her foot in the stirrup and heaved herself into the saddle.

"Goodbye for now, Agnes. I must find Freddie. I may see you tomorrow. If I can get away mayhap I will come to the fair."

Agnes stood and watched her ride away across the green.

'How like her father she is, such a kind heart, always ready to help less fortunate souls,' she thought.

Kate, unaware of several pairs of eyes watching her progress across the green, arrived at the cottage next to the inn and reined in her horse. An elderly woman was sitting on a stool in front of her open door busily sewing a patch on a skirt. She looked up as Kate slid from her horse. On seeing who her visitor was she hastily tried to get to her feet, only to be held back by Kate's hand.

"No, please do not rise," Kate smiled, "I believe it is your grandson I wish to see."

"Freddie?" queried Dorrit Clark.

"That is correct Mrs. Clark. Your little grand-daughter showed me a bird which she said her uncle had carved for her. It is so beautiful. Do you think he would sell me one?"

"Corse 'e wud," she said. "But yer can ask 'im yerself. Hare he cums now."

Kate turned around ready to greet the man coming up behind her. The smile on her face vanished as the man shambled awkwardly towards her. A feeling of revulsion shook her slender frame. Freddie stood facing her, a short thick set man with arms that were too long for his height. It was his face that had sent the cold chill through Kate. Two almond shaped eyes peered short-sightedly from deep set sockets. His mouth, from which his tongue kept flicking in and out, was thick lipped and saliva dribbled down his chin. Once the initial shock had passed,

Kate's natural compassion returned and she held out a hand. Freddie not understanding looked at his grandmother for help.

"The lady wants to shake yer 'and," she told him. "Are yer 'ands clean?"

Freddie gave a kind of grunt and wiped his hands down his smock then thrust one towards Kate.

"I am very pleased to meet you Mr., er, Freddie. Your niece, Betty, has told me how clever you are with those hands and I have come to see if you will sell me one of your animals."

Freddie looked down at his hands, staring at them as if he had not noticed them before, then he shambled off into the house.

Dorrit looked up at Kate, a smile on her care worn face.

"Thankyer fer that," she said. "A lot o' folks are skeerd of 'im and the children call'im nairmes and pelt 'im. 'E can't understand why. 'E's such a loveable man an' onla wants ter jine in their play."

Kate patted Dorrit on her thin shoulder and was about to speak when Freddie came out again carrying a box. Setting it down carefully on a stone slab by the gateway, he indicated by a series of grunts and hand-wavings that Kate should open the lid. She did so and gasped aloud at what she saw within. The box contained a t least thirty small birds and animals all so life-like that she was spellbound.

"How can I possibly choose one from this collection?" she murmured, picking up first one and then another. "They are all so beautiful."

Freddie seeing her dilemma picked up the box and thrust it before her with a large beaming smile. Kate glanced swiftly at Dorrit, who said softly, "he wants yer to 'ave 'em."

Kate gasped. "Oh, I could not take them all, that would be extremely greedy."

She fingered the animals again and then suddenly making up her mind picked out a horse.

"I will have this one for myself," she stated. "If I may I will take six more for the girls who work with Betty."

So saying, she picked out a frog, a cat, a dog, an owl, a wren and a cockerel, and as an afterthought, she pulled out a duck.

"The duck I will give to Nella," she explained, "she adores ducks. They have such happy faces she says. Now how much money do I owe you?"

Freddie looked shocked and shook his head vehemently.

"Y-You have…." he stammered.

"I must pay you," Kate explained. "You need clothes and food and to buy wood to make more. Please take these and keep them safe."

So saying she dropped a collection of gold and silver coins into his hand and smiled at both their astonished faces.

"Now I must depart," she said as they stuttered their thanks, and was putting her foot into the stirrup when a voice startled her saying…. "Allow me."

A pair of strong arms encircled her waist and she was hoisted up into the saddle. Glancing down she looked straight into the bright blue eyes of Tom Fullerton, and again she felt her heart hammering inside her rib cage. So loud did it sound to her that she felt sure he would hear it.

"Pardon the liberty my lady," he said, a smile lighting up his handsome, weather- browned face.

Unable to speak, Kate nodded and putting up a slender hand in a kind of wave, she set her horse to trot and made her way back to the Manor.

* * * * *

Colin was waiting by the derelict water mill as Kate approached just before noon. A bright smile lit up his sallow features as he saw her and helped her to dismount.

"We can sit on this green ridge," Kate said, "and the horses can be tied to that old post. They will be able to crop the grass while we talk."

"Will your gown not be spoilt if you sit on the grass?"

Kate grinned. "We have a good laundry lady who is used to my clothes getting dirty. My father was always saying that I should have been born a boy, and I was the bane of poor Nella's life."

Colin laughed and remarked that she must have had a happy childhood.

Kate sighed. "I did so until Father had to go away so much. Mother never had time for me – she preferred my brother Paul. He was always nice to me but was too old to play games. He is eight years older than me."

Colin took her hand.

"Where is Paul now?"

Kate sat staring with unseeing eyes into the clear running water of the little river.

"He is in Haarlem in Holland," she replied at last. "He married a Dutch girl whose father owns a linen mill and he helps to run it. Mother has been over to visit them once or twice but has never suggested that I accompany her."

Colin, who had been leaning back against the grassy bank, suddenly sat up.

"That's strange," he murmured.

"What is?"

"Father has also been on a few visits to Holland in these last few months."

Kate's face blanched.

"You think they may have gone together?" she asked.

"More than likely," he replied.

Kate got to her feet and brushed down the skirt of her dress.

"Oh I do so wish Father would come home," she stated. "I know people are laughing about Mamma and your father. My poor father will be mortified at her behaviour."

Colin nodded.

"I am ashamed of my father but Kate you do not know it all," he said, his face growing troubled. "You see, your mother is not his only paramour. He also visits Lady Dorothea Butters whose husband is lying sick abed of wounds received whilst fighting for King Charles, and there is another woman in Norwich whose husband is away with the Roundheads."

Kate's hands had flown to her trembling lips and tears came into her eyes. She ran down the slope to the water's edge and stood there trying to compose herself. Colin left her for a few moments, his own heart heavy with grief, then he went to her and placed his arms about her slim shoulders. After a few moments Kate turned her head to him.

"He is an evil man," she exclaimed. "Has he a purpose for keeping three ladies on a string?"

Colin nodded.

"He told me that whichever one was widowed first, that is the one he would marry. They are all rich women of course, but it is your mother that he hopes to wed, because of the two estates being side by side I suppose."

Kate's face was now as red as the poppies growing in the grass around their feet.

"How dare he?" she demanded hotly. "I shall write to my father immediately and send someone to London to find his whereabouts."

Together, the young couple strolled along the river bank letting the gentle lapping of the water ease the tensions in their heads. They watched little fish darting this way and that and were amused by the antics of a pair of water-hens. Suddenly a kingfisher dived into the water and surfaced again with a fish in his beak. They marvelled at the beauty of such a small bird. Silently they walked along skirting the small wood and passing the disused water mill until Colin suddenly came to a halt, a worried expression on his face.

"I must get back," he stated. "Father says I am to accompany him to Norwich. He wishes to leave by four of the clock and I shall be in dire trouble if I am not ready."

Kate's face fell as she looked at him.

"Oh dear," she said. "Will you be gone long?"

"About three days I think. He says he has business to attend to and wants to introduce me to some of his friends whom he says will instruct me in manly pursuits. I have no idea what he means by this but can only guess that it will not be pleasant because of the fiendish laughter which accompanied his speech."

"What a shame Colin," Kate said, taking his hand in hers. "There is a fair in the village tomorrow and I was going to ask you to take me there."

"Nothing would have pleased me more," he said, as they retraced their steps to where they had tied up their horses.

Kate handed Colin the pots of cream with instructions as to their use and then, after he had planted a kiss upon her hand, she watched sadly as he mounted and rode swiftly away.

* * * * *

The day of the fair dawned bright and clear, and an air of expectancy and excitement hung around the house. The servants scuttled to and fro about their various tasks and in the yard the milkmaids and the grooms were laughing gaily as they fed their animals. The chickens and ducks squawked and fled in panic, unused to the speed with which the men and girls were doing their chores. Even the dogs took to their heels and hid in the barn, peeping out occasionally to see if things had quietened down. Kate sat at the window of her attic room and watched the to-ings and fro-ings with great amusement.

Suddenly Cook appeared waving a wooden spoon.

"Cum you on in an' git yer breakfasts!" she yelled. "Stop yer shinanikins yer leary lot. Enna win 'ud think yer'd nivver bin to a fair afore."

This speech was greeted by loud laughter and promises that they would be in shortly.

"Dunt blairme me if yer porridge is cold," Cook said, and stamped off into the kitchen.

The staff had been informed the evening before that they could have time off to attend the fete and a two hour rota had been worked out. Kate walked along the corridor to check on the servants' rooms and was amazed to see Jed already busy with his paintbrush in the room next to the one he had done for Betty. Pushing open the door to Betty's room Kate stepped inside and looked around with astonishment. The walls gleamed white and made the room look much bigger.

'All it needs now is a little home comfort,' she thought to herself.

"You have done well Jed," she said smiling. "Did you scrub the floor too?"

Jed shook his paint splattered head.

"Not all onnit Miss. Betty did the moost."

"It looks very nice," Kate told him. "At this rate you will have all the rooms finished by the end of next week. The girls will be pleased but if you're going to the fair give yourself time to get cleaned up won't you."

"Ooh yis Miss. I'll git there, got er win me little sisters a necklace, oi hev."

Kate laughed and made her way down to her bedchamber where she found Nella tidying the bedclothes.

"Jed is doing a wonderful job upstairs," Kate told her. "When all the rooms are painted and scrubbed, we will fetch the bedside mats from the spare rooms in the west wing and then the girls will not step out of bed onto a cold floor when winter comes. I shall give each girl one of my paintings to hang on her wall and then we shall see about some decent furniture."

Nella raised her hands in mock horror.

"Go steady," she advised smiling. "Your mamma will throw a fit."

Kate shrugged her shoulders.

"She will not know unless she hears furniture being moved about, and anyway, I shall take full responsibility. Now Nella what can I wear this afternoon?"

For the next half an hour Kate tried on all the gowns in her massive wardrobe but all were discarded as being much too fancy.

"What am I going to do?" she wailed.

"Don't worry my dear," Nella said smiling gently. "We'll think of something. If only you'd had a suitable escort this problem would not have arisen. A young girl in your position cannot visit such a function unattended."

"Can you not come with me?"

"Sorry dear but with half the servants away I must stay here. But listen I have just thought of an idea."

About two hours later Kate was skipping along the lane accompanied by Betty, Flo, Sue and Jed. The young ones were so excited and inclined to run that Kate had great difficulty keeping pace with them and had to laughingly admonish them to calm them down. Kate's appearance had caused them great merriment but they were soon sworn to secrecy. Kate's own father would have had difficulty recognising her – so different did she look. Nella had found one of her oldest gowns and since they were very much the same size, little needed altering. Kate's lovely golden hair was braided up and pinned around her head and a servant's cap covered it all. The gown was a dull grey so they had livened it up with a colourful shawl. Little Jed had appointed himself Kate's protector and was trotting along beside her chattering away happily as they neared the village. The green, when they reached it, was a blaze of colourful activity. Several gypsy vardas stood on the roadway by the church and Kate was beckoned by one gypsy woman whom she could see had a crystal ball on the table before her.

"Tell yer fortune Lady?" the old woman cried.

"Perhaps later," Kate replied, giving her a warm smile then walked on past pedlars selling all kinds of cheap gewgaws. One woman Kate noticed had a collection of multi-coloured ribbons and narrow lace. 'I will buy some ribbons for the girls before we go home,' she thought.

Betty had spotted her mother in the crowd and having asked Kate's permission had run off to join her, taking Sue with her. Flo shortly became engrossed watching a group of acrobats so Kate walked with little Jed until they came almost to the inn. A rough platform had been erected there and a small band of musicians were preparing to play for dancing. Kate stood watching the colourful scene. Couples began to form a ring around part of the green. The music began and the boys and girls danced with great agility. She noticed Sue had found herself a partner, a brown haired boy aged about fifteen. Jed stood by Kate's side watching as she tapped her foot in time with the music.

"This wun is easy Miss," he informed her. "Would yer loike ter try?"

Kate was about to refuse but looking down into his eager little face she changed her mind.

"Certainly Sir," she replied and catching hold of his hands they joined the others, their laughter mingling with the happy throng until the music ceased.

"My turn now methinks," said a voice behind them. Kate startled, turned and found herself facing Tom Fullerton. At once her legs turned to jelly and her heart skipped a beat.

"I-I cannot do this dance," she stammered.

"You don't know what it is yet," laughed Tom. "Anyhow I will soon teach you."

Kate could see it was useless to refuse and anyway she knew she wanted contact with this handsome young man. Jed had other ideas!

"She's moi partner," he glowered. "Oim looking arter her."

Tom looked down.

"Oh it's you, young Jed," he said laughing. "Well I'm sure you'd rather go and watch the wrestling on the river. I'll take great care of your young lady."

Kate could not help but smile and she nodded her head to Jed as he looked up at her undecidedly. Then looking at Tom he suddenly made up his mind and trotted off down to the river where rafts had been anchored mid-stream for the wrestling.

"Now," said Tom, "give me your hands."

At first Kate hesitated, then she placed her hands in his. A shiver ran down her spine and the jelly in her legs turned to water. She felt as though she was floating. Somehow Kate managed to walk the few steps to join the circle of dancers and awaited instructions from Tom.

"Keep your hands in mine and when the music begins we glide four steps to the right and then four back again. Then I shall twirl you around and hand you to the next man in the line.

That's all there is to it but at the end of the dance you will get a surprise."

"What sort of surprise?"

"It wouldn't be a surprise if I told you, would it?" laughed Tom.

The music began and they were away. Kate began to enjoy herself even though she was dancing with farm workers from around Marley, including some of the staff from the Manor.

"Whatever would Mama say if she saw me?" she thought.

The music ceased and coming round from the last twirl she found herself once more facing Tom.

"So where is my surprise?"

"Close your eyes and you shall have it."

Kate did as bidden. Tom tilted her chin upwards and kissed her soft lips, a long lingering kiss that neither of them wanted to end. At last, with a sigh he released her and she was relieved to see that most of the other couples were engaged in the same activity.

"You dance very well and you kiss even better," Tom told her causing a hot flush to suffuse her face.

"How did it happen that you were opposite me at the end of the dance?" Kate enquired. "It could have been anyone."

Tom's laughter rang out.

"Not when I had promised to buy them a drink if they stopped when I got round to you again."

Kate tried to look cross but failed.

"You are incorrigible," she said, giving his arm a shake.

"More than likely," he said, adding mischievously, "that's if I knew what it meant!"

Kate's laughter rang out causing several heads to turn in their direction.

Tom, still grinning, took her arm and steered her towards the inn and they settled on rough chairs placed outside where customers could watch the merrymaking and enjoy a cooling drink. Kate sat back sipping a glass of ale and watched the colourful scene before her. Tom just sat and watched Kate!

The dancing was still continuing and other activities were taking place round about. A tug of war was causing great interest at the far end of the green and bobbing for apples in a tank of water was attracting a big group of youngsters. Kate could see Betty, her dress front dripping wet but joyfully holding aloft an apple she had grabbed with her teeth. Boys were kicking a blown up pig's bladder around, trying to get it between two sticks stuck up in the ground. Whoever managed this feat was given a small coin. Kate spotted a little figure leaning disconsolately against a stall watching them and she could tell by his manner that he was trying hard not to cry. Kate put down her now empty glass and with a quick explanation to Tom she made her way towards Jed. Jed saw her as she neared him and quickly drew his shirt sleeve across his face.

"What's wrong?" asked Kate. Jed shook his head and looked at the ground.

"Has someone been unkind to you?"

"No Miss."

"Then tell me," urged Kate, putting her arms about the boy's thin shoulders. Again he shook his head.

Tom, who had followed Kate, went over to the boy who had been playing and spoke to him. Kate saw the boy glance across at Jed and then he bent down and took off his well-worn boots. Tom picked up the boots and carried them across to Jed.

"There you are young Jed," he said, "now you can go and have a kick. That's what you wanted isn't it?"

Jed nodded, the tears again running down his face, but this time tears of happiness. The boots were quickly put on and laced up and Jed ran off to join the others.

"How clever of you to realise Jed's need," remarked Kate.

Tom grinned.

"Not really clever," he said. "He couldn't join the others because although his feet must be well hardened, to kick the bladder you use your toes and that hurts with no protection."

"Well thank you Tom," Kate said, blushing. Turning to the boys, she called over to Jed. "Only fifteen more minutes, Jed.

When the church clock strikes three we must be on our way."

Jed waved his hand and Tom and Kate left him there and walked around the green. When they reached the fortune teller Kate asked Tom to wait and she sat down before her. The gypsy woman took Kate's proffered coin, took the crystal into her hands and stared intently into it. For quite a while she was silent but with a worried frown upon her brown face she spoke at last.

"I do not like what I see Missy. It tells me that for a year or two you will be very happy but then you will have great sorrow. The glass clouds and I see no more."

Kate thanked the gypsy and rejoined Tom who had overheard the gypsy's forecast.

"Don't worry," Tom said, "a lot of these fortune tellers are just doing it for the money they take."

"Perhaps," replied Kate, but in her heart she felt that the old lady had seen something terrible. Giving herself a quick shake, she smilingly turned to Tom.

"I must get some ribbons from that girl over there and then I may have time to have a quick word with some of the cottagers before we leave." Tom took her arm.

"Do you have to leave so early Miss Ashe?" he asked with one of his cheeky grins.

"Oh! How long have you known?" she asked, blushing profusely.

"Ever since I looked into those incredible green eyes of yours," he admitted with a laugh.

Kate joined in his laughter and together they began to walk to where a group of village women were standing with the dancers. As the dance ended a clatters of horses' hooves was heard and people began to scatter at the far end of the green.

"Roundheads," breathed Tom, "I wonder what they want?"

There were five men, all riding big brown horses. They rode onto the green, not caring that they were knocking down pretty pennants that the villages had carefully hung around. One man, who appeared to be the officer in charge, jumped down and was soon in conversation with a group of men who were preparing to take part in a tug-of-war. Tom and Kate watched as the men nodded or shook their heads and they could see the Roundhead getting more and more agitated and his angry bellows reached their ears. One of the other men put his foot out and pushed over one of the stalls and this brought forth laughter from his companions who immediately began to follow his lead and so began a burst of noisy vandalism. Those villagers who dare to upbraid the Roundheads were kicked away or beaten across the head. The church clock struck three times and four figures raced towards Kate.

"Miss, Miss," panted Sue, as she slowed to a halt, "you'd better git hoom quick, them men says as ow they are lookin fer Sir Denzil. They sez as 'ow he wuz seen headin' this way."

Kate gave Tom a worried look. Swiftly he pulled her into the churchyard, out of sight of the commotion on the green. The servant girls and Jed followed.

"You'd best not go by the road or they'll overtake you," said Tom. "Do you know the short cut over the fields?"

Kate shook her head.

"I do," said Jed excitedly. "Oi'll show yer."

"Good," said Tom. "Off you go then. I will try to keep those ruffians here for as long as possible." So saying he ran back onto the green.

"You lead the way Jed," instructed Kate. The boy scampered off through the churchyard towards the back wall where he indicated a small gap in the brickwork. The girls wriggled through quite easily but Kate, being hampered by her skirts, had to be unceremoniously hauled through by the others. This hurdle surmounted they set off across a meadow scattering sheep as they went and then into a field of growing barley. Jed kept to the perimeter of the field so as not to harm the crop and soon they were in another meadow smelling sweetly of clover. Kate could see now that they were heading in the direction of the barn-yard and breathed a sigh of relief as they pulled up at the side of the milking shed.

"Thank you Jed," she smiled gratefully at the small able-footed boy.

Jed flushed shyly, then going to the end of the shed he looked about the yard.

"It's orlright, no-one about," he said.

"Good," said Kate. "You girls can explain to Cook what has happened and I shall go upstairs by the back staircase and get changed."

Nella was sitting embroidering a petticoat when Kate entered the bed chamber.

"My goodness," she exclaimed. "What have you been doing? You are all cobwebs and flower pollen!"

"No time to explain now, Nella. We have visitors calling shortly. Can you get me presentable please?"

Nella set to work and in a very few minutes Kate had had her grubby gown removed, had had a wash in rose water, dressed in a pink, flower-sprigged gown and was having the tangles brushed from her hair when they heard a loud banging on the front door.

"Would you answer that please?" asked Kate. Nella nodded and made her way downstairs. Kate finished brushing her hair and then slowly descended the stairs where she found Nella having an altercation with the Roundhead officer.

"We know he was here," he bawled. "He was seen yesterday only three miles away. So where is he?"

Nella shook her head.

"We have not seen Sir Denzil for almost two years," she said.

"Lying bitch!"

A leather gloved hand struck Nella viciously on the side of her head. (It was after this that she began to lose her hearing.)

"How dare you?" screamed Kate.

The men turned to see Kate at the bottom of the stairs and just at that moment Lady Maria appeared at the top.

"What is all this commotion?" she demanded.

"It is alright Mama. These, er, gentlemen seem to think we have hidden Papa."

"He cannot have vanished into thin air," the burly officer said through gritted teeth. "You have a priest hole somewhere in this house we have been told."

"Oh really? I wonder where you obtained that information?"

"Never you mind Miss Hoity Toity. Now are you going to show us where it is, or do you want us to tear the place down brick by brick?"

Kate smiled.

"No need for that. I will show you."

"Kate," Lady Maria cried, as Kate crossed to the fireplace at the end of the hall.

"It is quite alright Mama."

A very ornate wooden mantle carved with cherubs, fruit and leaves surrounded the fireplace and Kate, making sure that the men could not see, twisted one of the grapes. With a growling noise a bookcase to the left of the fireplace slowly slid outward, revealing a small empty chamber.

"There, you see," said Kate. "Nothing but dust and cobwebs. It has not been used since the days of Henry VIII."

The Roundheads roughly pushed her aside and began banging on the walls of the chamber, even using their knives to see if they could find a hollow spot. Eventually, their leader became impatient.

"Get upstairs and search every room and cupboard," he ordered. "You, Brown, come with me, we'll go downstairs."

Kate and Nella followed the men upstairs and went into Kate's bedchamber. They could hear the men banging on walls and throwing objects about, swearing as they did so. Soon, they entered Kate's rooms and she could feel her heart thumping as one of the men opened the doors to her wardrobe. He flung some of the gowns to the floor.

"Do you mind?" cried Kate. "Those are *my* gowns and now they will have to be laundered again. You can see no-one is hiding in there."

The Roundhead scowled but left the wardrobe and gave his attention to the bed. Finding nothing he left the room and joined the others.

"Thank the Lord for His goodness," said Kate. "I really thought that horrible man would find our secret."

Nella nodded. Kate noticed she was holding the side of her head and wincing as if in pain.

"Nella," she cried, "lie down on my bed and I will fetch something to ease your pain."

"It's alright, Kate, just a headache but I will lie down for a while if you don't mind."

Kate led Nella to the bed and pulled a woollen coverlet over her. Crossing to the window she peered out and could see the Roundheads searching the outbuildings, throwing out straw and hay and anything else that got in their way. The workmen in the yard were doing their best to prevent them doing too much damage but were getting kicked for their trouble. Jenny, the milk-maid came out of the cow byre, crying, two almost empty pails hanging from the yoke across her shoulders.

"If only I had been born a boy," Kate muttered to herself.

Soon the men, finding nothing, remounted their horses and rode off across the fields to the wood, and onwards towards Monksleigh Hall.

Kate glanced towards the bed and saw that Nella had fallen asleep. Going softly across the room to her wardrobe, Kate opened the door and pressed on a panel which immediately slid sideways, revealing stairs leading downwards. Closing the panel behind her she began to descend the narrow staircase. It was very dark but Kate had used these stairs many times so was quite familiar with every step. She had found the secret passage when only ten years old and had been playing "Hide and Seek" with Nella. Tripping over some clothing she had put out a hand to save her herself from falling and had accidently pushed the panel, revealing the stairs. Sir Denzil had been summoned and he had taken a candle and had explored the passage. Only Kate, Nella and Sir Denzil knew of its existence. Sir Denzil had explained that it might be very useful one day. Lady Maria was not informed because they were afraid she would tell all her card playing friends!

The stairs finished at what looked like a blank wall but Kate felt down the right side panel, found a button, pressed it and a door opened into a private little chapel. Kate blinked several times to get used to the light which was coming from a lighted candle on the little alter.

"Papa," Kate whispered, "are you here?"

A strong pair of arms enveloped her from behind and she twisted around to gaze into her beloved father's face.

"I guessed you would be here," she said, tears of joy rolling down her face. "However did you find the outside door?"

"I had to forcibly push a thick growth of ivy back but the key was still hidden in its usual place."

"Oh Papa, it is so good to see you again. We thought you must be dead. Where have you been all this time?"

"Hush dearest, all in good time. Is it safe to go upstairs?"

Kate nodded.

"There have been Roundheads here but they left before I came looking for you."

They made their way as silently as possible up the stairs and hesitated a moment or two before opening the panel and stepping into Kate's bedchamber. Nella was just awakening from her sleep and quickly rose to her feet as she saw Sir Denzil.

"Sir," she exclaimed and would have sunk to her knees in a curtsey had he not have taken her hands in his and drawn her upwards where he kissed her cheek before releasing her.

"Thank you for looking after this precious child in my absence," he said, bringing a flush to Nella's cheeks.

"My pleasure, Sir Denzil," she answered.

* * * * *

Some time later they were all seated in Lady Maria's salon drinking tea and listening to Sir Denzil's hair raising account of his adventures.

After King Charles had lost the battle of Naseby, Sir Denzil was given the dangerous honour of escorting Queen Henrietta

Maria to seek safety in her homeland of France. With her went the royal children and the queen's dwarf, a very small man who had become a favourite at Court and who had been knighted by King Charles. For some time Sir Denzil had remained in France carrying out his diplomatic duties. Returning to London he found the Parliamentarians had put a price on his head and so his life had consisted of dodging from one friend to another until he had at last reached his home.

"So what happens now?" demanded Lady Maria. "Are you staying?"

Sir Denzil, who was sitting softly stroking his dark pointed Van Dyke styled beard, sadly shook his head.

"I dare not stay Maria, those soldiers will be back. Not only will they arrest me, but Kate and you also if they find me here. As soon as it grows dark I must be on my way."

"Oh no," cried Kate, jumping to her feet so suddenly that she knocked the tea tray to the floor.

"Look what you have done you clumsy girl," snapped Lady Maria. "Ring the bell for a servant."

"I will clear it up," said Nella quietly, rising from her seat at the back of the room where she had been sitting with Lady Maria's companion.

"Papa," cried Kate, "we can hide you, please stay – at least for a few days."

Sir Denzil shook his head, the movement making his fashionable ringlets swing.

"I dare not, my dearest daughter, but I will return all being well, very shortly after I have fulfilled the duties entrusted to me. Come let us not be too melancholy, tell me what has been happening to you."

* * * * *

Kate had explained to her father about the plight of the servants and what she was doing to make their rooms more comfortable. Lady Maria was peeved that Sir Denzil condoned Kate's actions and flounced out of the room in a temper ordering her companion to follow.

"Come and see what we have accomplished so far," cried Kate excitedly, pulling Sir Denzil's hand. Chattering merrily she led the way upstairs to the attic rooms and pushed open the door to Betty's room.

"Now come and see the state of the other rooms, the ones not yet done."

Sir Denzil gasped in dismay as he inspected them.

"I had no idea things had got this bad," he said. "Surely the money I sent your Mamma was sufficient to house our servants properly. I will have words with her on the subject before I leave."

Just then a paint splattered figure emerged from one of the rooms. Jed stopped abruptly on seeing a strange gentleman in the corridor with Kate. Not knowing what to do he just stood there open mouthed, a frightened expression on his face.

"It is quite alright Jed. This is my father, Sir Denzil, no need to be afraid. I have been showing him your handiwork," Kate said, smiling.

Sir Denzil stared at the little form before him.

"So you are the painter are you?" he questioned kindly.

"Yis Sir, thank yer kin'ly sir," Jed managed to mutter.

"And do you always paint barefooted?" asked Sir Denzil.

Jed hung his head.

"Hent got no shoes."

Sir Denzil looked at Kate.

"This we will soon remedy," he said. "Follow me – and you Nella."

Kate, Nella and a bewildered Jed followed Sir Denzil along the corridor and into the West Wing of the manor. At the very last door he turned the handle and entered. They found themselves in a large storeroom packed full with cupboards and crates.

"This room is full of Paul's cast off clothing. He will never need any of it now. Somewhere there must be a collection of shoes and boots, so come along let us search."

Kate was getting more and more excited as she opened boxes and crates full of boys' clothing.

"Look Jed," she cried, holding aloft a pair of brown breeches, "these would fit you nicely."

At that moment Nella opened a large wall mounted cupboard and there inside were the shoes. Dozens of pairs all neatly arranged in sizes starting from babyhood up to the time Paul had left to live in Holland. Some had gone a bit green due to dampness but Nella said that could be remedied.

"Come along young man," ordered Sir Denzil, " let us see if we can fit you up."

Jed, whose eyes had widened at the sight of so many clothes and shoes, was lost for words but sat down obediently on a crate as Nella went to try a pair of strong boots on to his thin grubby feet. Sir Denzil had been delving into one of the crates which seemed to contain underwear. Triumphantly he pulled out several pairs of woollen hose.

"There we are lad. They will keep your legs and feet warm, looks as though the moths have had a dinner or two out of them though. Can your mother darn?"

Jed nodded, tears of joy running down his face.

"Th-thank yer, sir," he said "but kin 'oi give me brother a pair cus e feels the cold summat bad in winter. He ent strong y'see."

Sir Denzil looked at Kate.

"Do you know his family?"

"Only that besides his brother there are four sisters and his mother. The father was killed in this terrible war. They live in a hovel by the village green."

Sir Denzil chewed his bottom lip thoughtfully, then pulling out a leather pouch from inside his tunic he handed it to Kate and instructed her to attend to the family and repair the house and any other cottages in the village that were in disrepair. Kate was also given permission to take anything from the storeroom to clothe any of the other needy servants.

Later that evening when it was almost dark a grateful little boy led Sir Denzil across the fields to the house of the village priest where his horse had been stabled. After seeing his master safely on his way, Jed ran across the green to deliver a sack of clothing to his mother.

* * * * *

A few days later Kate was sitting in her favourite spot by the bubbling, meandering stream, where although only about half a mile from the manor house she was hidden by the slight rise of the bank behind her. Before her, over the stream, were fields belonging to Mill Farm, and she could see people busy at work. To her right some distance away was the mill, whilst to her left a bridleway led to woods and the ruined water mill. Quite absorbed in sketching the scene before her, Kate failed to notice that she was not alone until a slight cough made her start and jump to her feet. Turning, she saw Tom Fullerton grinning at her from the top of the bank.

"Oh it's you Mr. F-Fullerton," she stammered.

"Not so much of the Mr., if you please," he laughed. "My name is Tom."

So saying he jumped down from the bank and scrutinised the sketch Kate had been doing.

"Hmm – very good," he remarked. "You have great talent."

"Thank you," she blushingly replied, unable to meet his eyes. "Painting is my favourite hobby."

Tom nodded. Kate resumed her seat on the lush green grass and continued her sketching.

"Tell me, Tom, what are those people doing over there?"

Tom looked to where she was pointing.

"Ah they are pulling up the flax. Did you know that flax is the most useful crop to grow?"

Kate shook her head.

"I only know that it's the most beautiful shade of blue when in flower."

Tom agreed and went on to explain.

"It is now ripe enough to harvest. Each stem has to be pulled out separately because the longer the stem the finer the fibres. After it has been taken to the barn and the seed heads cut off, the women will sew the stalks together to form a kind of mattress. Then they bring them down and put them in the river."

Seeing Kate's puzzled face he went on. "They are left there until the stalks are soft enough to pull apart. Each stem contains many fibres and these have to be carefully pulled from the stem, very hard on the hands. We call this scutching. Then the flax fibres are put into sacks and sent off to be made into linen."

Kate smiled.

"My brother, Paul, helps his father-in-law run a linen mill in Holland – but tell me why is flax so useful?"

Tom sat down beside her and explained.

"The seeds are full of oil and this oil can be used in lots of ways. Your furniture is probably polished with it. It is used in varnish and in soap. The meal that is left after the oil has been taken out can be eaten and a lot of it is given to animals. Agnes in the village uses it to make poultices to bring out thorns and such. She also uses it to make up a concoction to cure diarrhoea and to make cough cures."

"When the fibres are spun and woven the very finest are made into handkerchiefs and tablecloths and clothing, and of course, bed linen. The coarser fabric can be made into sails for boats and harnessing for horses. It also makes thread, twine and even rope."

"Short fibres cannot be made into cloth but can make paper and cleaning stuff. The chaff left from the stems is used to feed farm animals and even the duct can be used to manure fields. So you see Kate, that is why flax is the most useful of all plants. Not one piece of it is wasted."

Kate sat gazing at Tom as he was speaking and as he finished she said shyly, "Thank you, Tom. That was very interesting but will you tell me one more thing?"

"If I can."

"This is a little embarrassing – how is it you speak so well and with hardly any dialect at all? Have you been schooled?"

Tom laughed.

"No need to be embarrassed," he said. "The Rector in Marley taught me to read and write and since then I read every book I can lay my hands on – when I'm not working of course."

Kate was just about to offer to lend him some books from the Manor library when they heard hoof-beats and looking up saw Sir Colin Monksleigh coming towards them on his grey hunter.

Kate jumped to her feet and ran to meet him. He dismounted and they flung arms around each other and hugged. Kate having her back to Tom did not see the look of dismay that crossed his face but Colin noticed and wondered. Breaking apart from the embrace Kate drew Colin towards Tom and introduced the two young men, unaware of a frisson of jealousy between them.

"Tell us about Norwich," she told Colin and was amazed to see his face turn crimson.

"It was terrible," he blurted out after a short pause. "Father took me to a house. Pushed me inside and told me he would pick me up on the morrow."

Colin hung his head.

"I cannot tell you all, Kate. I was so embarrassed when I realised where Father had taken me."

Tom said quietly, "It was a brothel Sir?"

Colin nodded.

"As soon as I realised I picked up my jacket which one of the women had taken from me and ran out into the street. It seemed I ran for hours getting more and more lost. Then I came to a church and went in."

Colin paused, then looking at Kate's stricken face he went on.

"A priest came to me because he could see I was in distress and I told him my story. He let me stay at his house for two days and we had many long conversations. I told him I wished to become a priest and he is going to help me – but it may be some time. In the meantime he has lent me some books to study."

Kate smiled.

"Some good has come out of it after all," she said.

Tom had been listening silently. Suddenly he threw an arm around Colin's shoulders.

"Sir," he said, "I think I must take you in hand, teach you a little bit of self- defence, help build up your self-confidence so that you will no longer run away from difficulties but stand and face up to them."

Tom removed his arm smiling self-consciously.

"Sorry Sir," he said, "I'm forgetting my place."

"Oh please call me Colin, and I shall call you Tom. Any friend of Kate's is a friend also, and yes I would like you to give me lessons on self-defence. Can we begin on the morrow?"

"Of course. Meet me here tomorrow at four of the clock. Now, I see the cart is laden with sacks so I must away to take it to the barn."

So saying Tom waved a cheery goodbye to Kate and Colin and ran rapidly towards the bridge that spanned the river, which divided the land belonging to the mill farm and the fields belonging to the Manor.

"He seems a decent young man," remarked Colin, looking at Tom's retreating back.

"Yes, he is," answered Kate. "But now let me look at you."

Colin fidgeted a little as Kate studied his hair and face.

"There is a great improvement already," she said at last. "The spots are clearing and your hair is so much better. I am so pleased for you."

"Even my sisters have noticed the difference," he said. "I must get them some of the salves when they are a bit older."

Together they sat and watched the activity in the fields over the river. Kate picked up her forgotten sketch pad and added some of the workers to it including Tom as he led the horse and cart away to the old thatched barn.

The wide Norfolk sky was a beautiful blue with only a few fluffy white clouds to be seen. The birds in the nearby wood were chirruping happily and the grasshoppers in the grass by their feet rubbed their legs together to make their very distinctive sound. Colin caught one and held it gently in his hand for a moment.

Colin and Kate gazed at the strange little creature until with a leap it left Colin's hand and joined the others in the grass. A bittern boomed in the distance and was answered by another closer to hand. They heard the bark of a dog fox from somewhere in the wood and two wood pigeons cooed gently as they flew overhead. Colin lay back on the grass gazing skyward.

"It's so peaceful here," he sighed. "I wish that I could stay but I must get back home. Perhaps father has returned from Norwich."

Kate gasped.

"You mean he has not returned since you left that dreadful place?"

"I expect he has been at the gaming tables. He loses track of time when he gambles – not to mention getting drunk."

"Perhaps he is searching for you," Kate giggled.

"I think not Kate, but it would serve him right if he was. Anyhow I left a message for him at the livery stables where we left our horses, telling him that I had left for home. He will be in foul humour when he does get back so I must go and await him."

Colin got to his feet and assisted Kate to rise. After making arrangements to meet again the following day, the young couple went their separate ways.

* * * * *

All through the rest of that summer the young people met as often as they could. With Tom's help Colin learned to wrestle and shoot arrows into a target fixed to an old oak tree. They swam in the river and soon Colin was almost as brown and as strong as Tom, helped of course, by the meals Betsy cooked for him!

Kate envied the boys their freedom. How she would have loved to splash about in the river with them but had to be content to sit on the bank and watch. Tom noticed the longing looks she gave them and had an idea.

The following day when she joined them at the river she was surprised to see a raft moored there, complete with a large soft cushion. A rope fastened to one end was held by Colin, and Tom bowing low, smilingly instructed Kate to step aboard "the good ship *Katherine*".

And so Kate was able to feel more a part of their activities. They fished, had picnics and punted the raft along the river. When Tom was too busy on the farm to join them, Colin and Kate spent the long sultry days sitting on the grassy ridge, Kate sketching and Colin studying the books on theology, which the Norwich priest had lent him. Kate found herself growing more and more fond of both boys and wondered what the future had in store.

Kate and Colin announced their "betrothal" to a delighted Lord Monksleigh but had explained to Tom and Nella that it was only a pretence and would be broken as soon as Colin could leave for Norwich. The portrait of Kate had been completed and now hung in pride of place overlooking the carved oak staircase where visitors could see it as they entered the hall and ascended the stairs.

And so the year wore on. One of the happiest that Kate had experienced. News came through, via a messenger sent from Sir Denzil, that the war was over and that King Charles had surrendered to the Scots. Although Kate was sorry for the King she was happy too because some of the men from the village began to return home to rapturous welcomes from their families.

'If only Father could come home now,' she thought, 'my life would be complete.'

But that was not to be as Sir Denzil was advised not to return home as the Roundheads still hunted him. Christmas came and went, a joyous occasion for the families who had their fathers or sons home even though some of them were badly injured. Kate and Nella made sure that the families had sufficient food and even took them little gifts to open on Christmas Day. On New Year's Eve a special thanksgiving service was held in the village church and everyone who could attended. Even Lady

Maria, accompanied by her maid, condescended to put in an appearance. Making her entrance at least three minutes late she swept up the aisle, her skirts rustling on the stone floor. On reaching the front pew she signalled for Kate to move along and sat down smoothing her clothes around her as she did so. Then having decided she was comfortable she nodded to the priest to proceed, causing the large feather in her hat to wobble precariously. Kate had to put her hand to her mouth to hide a smile and she heard one or two giggles from the children at the back of the church. After a stimulating service Kate stood by her mother to distribute largesse to the villagers - a ritual started by Sir Denzil's father soon after the Manor was built. Each person came forward to receive their coin, bowed or curtsied, then left after wishing their benefactors a Happy New Year. The long line of people was almost to the end when Kate beheld a brown hand and glancing up looked into the blue eyes of Tom. Kate blushing, placed the coin into his palm, but before she could remove her hand Tom had closed his fingers around her slender hand. Again Kate felt that tingle go through her body – just as she had on that first meeting on the village green.

"You look very beautiful today Miss Ashe," he whispered and before she could speak his hand was removed from hers and Tom was gone.

Kate glanced quickly at her mother but she was engaged in conversation with Giles Fordham, the village priest, and so had seen nothing. Nella, however, had witnessed the tender little incident and on arriving home and once more ensconced in Kate's room she began to question her.

"You are not getting too fond of young Tom Fullerton are you Kate?" she began.

Kate gazed dreamily into the blazing fire lit by Nella on their return from church.

"I am very fond of him Nella – but I am also fond of Colin. They have become such good friends to me."

Nella crossed the room and sitting beside Kate she took the young girl's hand in hers.

"You must be careful not to become too fond of either of them," she warned. "Only a broken heart can be the result. Colin has a title but no money and intends to become a priest and Tom is only a poor farmer's son. So Kate, you must see that life with either of them would be impossible."

Tears shone in Kate's eyes.

"I am not contemplating marrying anyone just yet," she cried, "they are both my very dear friends."

Nella drew Kate into her arms.

"Good," she said, "that is the way it must be. One day you will find someone suitable to love."

"How shall I know when I fall in love?" Kate asked.

Smilingly Nella answered, "You will know Kate, believe me, you will know."

Kate drew back and looked into Nella's face.

"Have you ever been in love Nella?" she asked.

"Yes, dearest girl. I have known love. Deep lasting, tender love."

Kate's face registered her astonishment.

"But what happened? Why did you not marry?"

"He already had a wife my dear, and although the marriage was not a happy one,he was a Catholic and could not go against his faith."

"Oh poor Nella," Kate cried, hugging her, tears welling in her beautiful eyes.

Nella took out her kerchief and gently dabbed the tears away.

"Do not fret for me Kate," she said. "I have been very happy here looking after you – now come we must freshen up and partake of the luncheon that Betsy has prepared. Did you not say that Colin and Lord Monksleigh were invited?"

Kate jumped to her feet.

"Nella I had forgotten. I must hurry." So saying she rushed into the little ante- room off her bedchamber.

* * * * *

During the next two months Kate saw little of either of her young friends. The weather was atrocious all through January and February. After severe snow falls and frosts the thaw brought floods and most of the village was cut off when the river overflowed. The children were thrilled and spent their days paddling and boating in the dirty cold water much to their mothers' chagrin. The older ones, wrapped in old sacking to keep out the cold, helped the men to move hay and other animal feeds onto higher benches in the barns. The sheep almost due to lamb had to be brought in before they drowned in the waterlogged fields. Kate was able to watch all the activity from her attic room window and sometimes caught a glimpse of Tom as he fought to save his own flock from drowning. When the water had subsided, Colin managed to ride through the mud to the manor and the young people spent a happy afternoon together.

"Father is pestering me to set a wedding date," Colin told Kate.

A look of alarm spread across Kate's face.

"Did you tell him we are in no hurry?" she asked. Colin nodded.

"I told him that we will not marry until Sir Denzil is here to give you away."

Kate breathed a sigh of relief.

"They cannot make us marry can they?"

"No Kate, we are both under age."

"You have not changed your mind about becoming a priest have you?"

"No Kate, but there have been occasions when I have looked at your lovely face and wondered if I am doing the right thing."

Kate laughed and rose from her seat by the window.

"You are a tonic Colin," she said, "but look outside, darkness is falling. You must go before you cannot see the ruts in the road. We do not want your horse to take a tumble."

She led Colin to the kitchen door and gave him a quick kiss on his cheek. Colin rode home, his heart hammering. One hand holding the reins, the other pressed against his cheek where Kate had planted the kiss.

And so the weeks flew by. Spring meant a great upheaval in the manor house. Curtains were brushed down, carpets and rugs taken outside and thoroughly beaten. Floors and furniture polished with beeswax – made by Betsy – until they gleamed. Windows had to be cleaned inside and out to rid them of the winter's grime and the droppings of the doves which lived in the dove-cote.

Lady Maria took her companion to spend a few days with her sister at Cromer whilst all this was taking place. The dust caused her to have asthma attacks she complained. Once the house was again spick and span, the servants and Kate raided the gardens for sweet smelling flowers and herbs and every vase in the house was utilised.

Kate and Nella stood looking at their handiwork.

"It is beautiful," said Kate, clasping her hands together ecstatically. "Just smell those gilly flowers in the hearth."

Nella nodded.

"And the roses in the jardinières by the staircase," she remarked.

Together they walked from room to room admiring their labours.

"The servants have worked really hard and deserve some reward," Kate stated. "We will have a party and all shall attend – even Colin and Tom if they can get away."

Nella smiled, her hand upon her ear. It had been hurting quite a lot recently and she had suffered quite a loss of hearing. Kate's enthusiasm was catching however, so forgetting her pain she joined in arranging a get together for the staff.

Betsy was consulted and was keen to help.

They thought the Saturday would be the most suitable day as that gave them two days for cooking and preparing everything. Saturday dawned, and turned into a warm spring day, so it was decided to take trestle tables out onto the lawn where there would be more room. Molly, Betty and Sue dashed excitedly back and forth from the kitchen to tables and soon the tables groaned under the weight of the food the girls placed upon them. There were roast chickens and ducks, slices of pork and lamb, savoury pies and fruit pies, new crusty bread and dishes piled high with sweetmeats. Nella and Kate had helped Betsy prepare some of the dishes – thoroughly enjoying themselves in the process.

During the afternoon Colin arrived on his horse and his eyes almost popped out of his head. He had never before seen such a spread. At four o'clock Betsy rang her brass bell and the servants, dressed in their Sunday best, ran out onto the lawn. Even the cowman and grooms had managed to get cleaned up and the farm labourers came too, standing shyly aside – not quite knowing what to do.

"Come along," Kate called. "Come and join the party. There is food and drink for all. Let our celebration begin."

At this, a group of musicians that Kate had hired for the occasion began to play and everyone started to relax and enjoy themselves. Kate and Nella assisted by Colin served out small tankards of beer and handed out pewter plates.

"Take your fill," instructed Kate. "You have worked hard and deserve a reward."

"Do I get a reward?" said a well-known voice in her ear.

"Tom!" she laughed, "I'm so glad you could come. Help yourself to meat. There is plenty for all."

"That is not what I meant," Tom answered, with one of his cheeky smiles. "I will claim my reward later."

So the festivities continued with dancing and singing, eating and drinking, until gradually some of the men had to leave to milk the cows and see to other animals in stables and sties. Kate and Nella with Betsy surveyed the remaining food on the tables.

"Whut ivver shell we do wirrit?" asked Betsy. "Moost onnit wunt keep til termorrer."

Just then little Jed walked by and Kate had an idea.

"We will do it up into packages and send it to the villagers who are needy," she said.

Shortly after, Jed and most of the servant girls were to be

seen heading for their homes, happily carrying parcels of food. The tables and trestles were soon cleared away and the bones and other residue picked up from the lawn. The musicians had helped with the clearing so Kate paid them well and they departed, each one with red cheeks – brought on no doubt by the copious tankards of beer they had drunk – rather than any overdue exertion. One hour later Lady Maria arrived home and life continued.

During June Sir Denzil paid an unexpected visit to the Manor much to the delight of Kate, Nella and the staff.

"Father, it is so good to see you," Kate told him as they strolled in the gardens where early flowers were blooming. "Will you stay long this time?"

Sir Denzil shook his head sadly.

"I fear not my dear. I must go to London to see where Parliament has imprisoned King Charles."

Kate's hands flew to her mouth as her face registered shock at the news.

"Imprisoned?" she cried. "What has his Majesty done that he is treated so?"

"It is a long story my dear," Sir Denzil replied. "Let us sit on this seat and I will try to explain it all to you."

So Kate learned about the King and his extravagances. How he believed that because he was anointed King he had a divine right to ask Parliament for money to fund his many skirmishes with Spain. When Parliament refused he dismissed all his ministers and tried to rule the country alone. This caused the Civil War and divided the country, the Loyalists supporting the King, and the Parliamentarians being led by Cromwell and Thomas Fairfax. In January Charles had been handed over to Cromwell by the Scots and held on house arrest at Holdenby in Northampstonshire. Here he lived more or less freely until recently when five hundred horsemen had arrived to escort him to London.

"Father," cried an astonished Kate, "is the King a bad man?"

"No dearest," Sir Denzil replied. "Just stubborn and foolish. He believes he has the God given right to ask for things and should be obeyed. He is extremely religious and spends hours praying for his country."

Kate listened, open-mouthed.

"So where were you when they came to take the King to London?" she asked.

"I lodged with friends at Althrop. Charles was allowed to visit there to play bowls and so we were able to talk. It was difficult though because there were always armed guards around him."

"So now you must follow him to London?"

"Yes Kate. Other Royalist friends will join me on the journey but we must be most careful. The Roundheads would love to capture us."

"Oh Father why do you have to go on such a dangerous mission?"

Sir Denzil laughed.

"Because my dear, the King is my friend and he trusts me to keep his Queen informed as to his whereabouts. Once I have located his Highness, I shall board a boat and away to France - so you see it will be a few weeks before I can return."

Kate laid her golden head on her father's shoulder and his arms came around her. They sat quietly on the garden seat for some time then they rose and went back into the house still tightly wrapped around each other.

Sir Denzil left early the following morning before even the staff was astir.

* * * * *

Kate resumed her activities on the river with Tom and Colin but this time with a difference. Whenever she went out to meet the young men Nella made sure that one of the servants accompanied her. Usually it was Jed. He was very proud of his new responsibility as chaperone to Miss Kate, and sat by the river watching the others as they fished or pulled Kate along on the raft. Most of all he liked to watch the archery because then Miss Kate sat beside him on the grass and watched the boys. One day Tom noticed Jed's intent face as he followed their every move.

"Like to have a go young Jed?" he called.

Jed looked up to Kate questionably.

"Go on Jed," she said smiling. "Let's see what you can do."

Jed hesitated.

"Miss Nella said not to leave you."

Kate grinned, showing perfect white teeth, and with a slight push sent him off to join the others. Tom chose one of the lightest arrows and after a little instruction Jed let fly at the rings cut out of the tree. His first arrow went wide but after a few more attempts he began to score.

"Well done," said Colin. "You have a natural aptitude for archery."

Jed, not quite sure what 'natural aptitude' meant, looked at Kate for enlightenment and after she had explained his little face was one large beam. Kate could not quite put a finger on it but this summer seemed different to the previous carefree one. There seemed to be an undercurrent of feelings between the boys, something akin to jealousy. Kate was at a loss to understand it, as she knew she treated them equally. Nella laughed when Kate mentioned the matter to her.

"Kate, my dearest," she said, "why do you think I send Jed or Betty with you when you go to the river? Last year you were children, this year you are adults. You have all had birthdays and the young men are vying for your attention. It is only natural. I think, my dear, that you must see less of them from now on."

Kate was horrified!

"Nella," she cried, "it is not that bad, and anyway Tom is having to spend more time on the farm so it will sort itself out. Colin and I are still unofficially betrothed so no one will consider it strange if I am seen with him until he goes off to Norwich."

Nella smiled and was about to speak when a commotion in the courtyard drew her attention. Kate, hearing horses' hooves clattering on the flag stones, dropped the embroidery she was doing and joined Nella at the window. A group of Roundheads were dismounting from their sweating, tired horses. They were shouting orders to the stable lads who had appeared from the barn where they had been loading a hand cart with straw prior to taking it in to the stable.

Nell and Kate watched as they took the soldiers' horses to the water trough and as they drank rubbed them down with old sacking. Jenny, the dairy maid and Jim Bland, the blacksmith, were busy settling a few bits of furniture into the rooms over stable. This was to be their future home after their marriage on the coming Saturday. Hearing the noise in the yard they ran quickly down the stone stairs – only to be confronted by a burly Roundhead.

"Aha," the man chortled, "and what is this I see? A fine wench methinks."

Jim tried to lead Jenny away but the soldier grabbed the girl's arm and with a mighty clout sent Jim reeling into a pool of muddy water.

"You come with me my beauty," the soldier said.

Jenny started struggling but the man's strength was too much for her and she was half dragged, half carried, screaming into the stable and the door slammed behind them. Jim got to his feet and attempted to go after them but was held back by two other Roundheads. Jenny's terrified screams lasted for several minutes punctuated by curses from the soldier and then silence. The door opened and the Roundhead emerged, his face raked with scratches. He grinned as he saw Jim being held by his friends.

"Your wench is she?" he sneered. "A right little vixen – but I've broken her in for you."

Jim tried to struggle free but unable to do so spat in the soldier's face. This earned him another blow to his head and when the soldiers released him he fell to the ground, semi-conscious.

Upstairs in Kate's attic room Nella enclosed a weeping Kate in her arms.

"We must go to her," Kate sobbed

"In a moment my dear, let those beasts go first. They are already mounting their horses."

Still laughing raucously the men rode off round the side of the Manor, down the driveway and onto the lane. Nella and Kate ran swiftly down the back stairs, through the kitchen and into the yard where most of the staff were congregating.

Looking at them Nella asked "Where is Betsy?"

"Gone to see to Jenny, Miss," answered Flo, sniffing back tears.

"Good," Nella replied. "Now all of you go on with your work. You, Betty, make sure there is plenty of hot water and I will join Betsy. Get along all of you."

Tearfully they moved away. Kate made to follow Nella as she went towards the stable but Nella restrained her saying, "No Kate. Wait here awhile until I see what sort of state she is in."

Joining a distraught Betsy, Nella looked down at the young girl lying unconscious in a pile of straw. Her dress, red stained and ripped apart, revealed the top part of her body. Already dark blue bruises showed up on her face where the brutish man had obviously beaten her, but worse still were the teeth marks on her breasts and neck.

"Is she dead Miss Nella?" asked Betsy, crying into the coarse apron she held to her eyes. Nella gently covered the young girl and felt for a pulse.

"No," she replied at last, "but we must get her into the house at once. Would you please fetch a shawl or something to wrap her in and get one of the men to carry her?"

Betsy nodded and ran off.

Meanwhile Kate had taken charge of Jim and was assisting two of the servant girls to bathe his swollen face. Jim seeing her tried to get to his feet to ask after Jenny but was held down by the girls. Betsy sped across the yard to where one of the workers was just coming after his day's labour.

"Quickly Bill," she ordered, "follow me to the stable."

Bill realising that something was amiss, dropped his tools

and followed her. Soon Jenny was wrapped in the cloak and Bill gathered up the limp form in his arms and the little party made their way towards the house.

"We will take her to my room," said Nella, as she opened the kitchen door. "This way Bill – I will show you the way. Betsy could you and one of the girls fill my bath-tub and bring towels?"

Betsy nodded and soon she and Betty were hurrying upstairs.

Jim, meanwhile, had recovered enough to go back to the smithy where he took his rage out on a red hot horseshoe. Bill found him there shortly after and told him that Miss Nella wished him to go to the village, tell Agnes what had happened and bring her back with some healing salves.

"Is Jenny bad?" asked Jim anxiously.

Bill nodded, his eyes moist. Jim wasted no time. Untying the horse that stood patiently waiting to be shod, he leapt onto its unsaddled back and set off across the fields. An hour or so later, Jenny, having been gently bathed by Nella and Kate, was clad in a soft white nightgown and was lying in Nella's bed. Agnes, having applied her salves was preparing to leave, re-opening her bag she took out a bottle.

"When she comes round," she instructed, "make her drink this – 'tis rue – rather nasty to drink but it will stop her gettin' with child."

Kate accompanied Agnes downstairs and after paying for the salves, thanked her profusely and let her out of the front door. Turning round she was confronted by an angry Lady Maria.

"What is going on here?" she demanded. "Cook tells me that she has not yet prepared dinner. You know I always have dinner at seven-thirty."

Kate, inwardly seething, replied.

"Mama, we have had a terrible afternoon. One of the maids was raped and nearly beaten to death by a Roundhead."

"That is no concern of mine," snapped Lady Maria. "Tell Cook to have dinner on the table immediately or she can pack her bag and go."

Lady Maria strode off angrily. Kate crossed the hall and

made for the kitchen. Betsy was making pastry for an apple pie. She looked up and brushed the hair from her face with a floury arm. Kate smiled sympathetically, knowing Betsy was tired out from all her exertions of the day. Her plumpness and the heat from the stove did not help.

"Can I help in any way?" Kate asked.

"Bless yer Miss Kate but I think we are coping. Betty remembered ter put the cockrul in the the oven so he'll be done. The stove is well 'ot so the pie'll not tek long. Edie is already settin' the table. It's just the soup I'm worried about."

Kate laughed.

"Worry no longer," she cried, "I will tell Mama it is too hot for soup today so we are having a salad instead. Molly and Betty come with me and we will see what we can find."

Soon they were back with a collection of greenery, which they washed and then dried. Following Betsy's instructions Kate made a bed of lettuce leaves in a large bowl and then placed on it young dandelion leaves, a little watercress, some finely chopped up carrots, wild garlic and then decorated it with nasturtium and daisy heads, sitting on slices of hard boiled eggs.

"There you are Betsy," she cried triumphantly. "Now a hunk of cheese and some of your lovely bread and we have a first course fit for a king."

Upstairs Jenny was beginning to stir and as Kate entered the room, she cried out with pain.

"S-sh dear," said Nella softly, "just lie still and the pain will ease." Jenny looked around the room.

"Wh-where am I?" she murmured.

"In my bed chamber," smiled Nella.

"But I cannot stay here."

"Of course you can," replied Nella. "I can use the day bed for tonight and tomorrow we will see if you are well enough to go home."

Tears ran down Jenny's cheeks.

"My mother will wonder where I am – and oh dear – what about the milkin'? It must be late, the sky is darkening."

Kate came forward and took the girl's hand in hers.

"You need not worry about the milking. The men said they could manage and your mother will be coming to see you very soon. We have sent her a message."

"You are very kind Miss Kate and you too Miss Nella, but how am I going to face everyone? I can't get married now. Jim won't want me."

Tears again ran down her face.

"Of course he will, Jenny," Kate said. "He is downstairs now pacing up and down, just waiting until he is called. He got hurt too you know, trying to defend you."

Jenny's face again crumpled and as Kate gently wiped away the tears, Nella came to the bed bearing a tumbler of the rue potion that Agnes had left.

"Drink this, my dear," she instructed. "Agnes says it is to prevent you becoming with child. She says it is nasty so see if you can drink it down quickly then I will get you some water to take the taste out of your mouth."

Pulling a face at the thought of the consequences – even that hurt – she took the tumbler and drank deeply.

"Would you like a bowl of soup?" asked Kate.

Jenny shook her head and sank her battered head into the feather pillows.

"Shall I tell Jim to come up?" asked Kate.

A look of apprehension crossed Jenny's face then, after hesitating for a moment, she nodded.

"I will stay with them until her mother comes," Nella whispered to Kate, as she let her out of the room. "I have a feeling that she may be sick."

Kate ran downstairs and informed Jim that he could go and visit Jenny but she warned him not to let her see shock on his face – shock that she knew he would feel when he looked at her injuries.

Hardly any food was eaten that night in the kitchen and most of the staff retired early.

*****

Several weeks later Kate was standing on the ridge looking out over the fields. Harvest was almost over. A few stocks of corn stood waiting to be pitch-forked into a cart ready to be taken away to the stack yard. Already some of the village women with their children were busily gleaning, picking up the odd heads of corn that had fallen from the stooks, and putting them into a sacking apron especially made for the purpose. The following day they would take their corn to the mill to be ground into flour and though it would not be much, the family could look forward to their dumplings or bread for a few days.

Kate could not help but compare herself with these hard working, old before their time, women and herself. Her kind heart felt for the women and the girls but she knew that the girls at the Manor and the families in the village were better looked after than others on neighbouring estates. Events of the past weeks came back to her as she stood there. The Reverend Giles Fordham had agreed to put off the ceremony until Jenny had recovered from her injuries. Now they had moved into the rooms over the stable and seemed very happy – but Kate wondered if Jenny would fully recover from her ordeal. From a bubbly carefree girl she now seemed subdued and nervy. 'Still time is young yet,' Kate thought. Sighing she began to walk slowly along the ridge, passed the ruined mill and came to the oak tree. Stopping in its shade she leaned back and gazed upwards into the branches. Some of the leaves were turning yellow she noticed. Soon they would become brown and fall to make a soft carpet around the tree. A squirrel caught her attention as it darted about looking for fallen acorns. So enraptured was she that she failed to hear footsteps approaching until a voice startled her.

"Ah, the lovely Miss Ashe," it said.

Kate turned her head.

"Lord Monksleigh," she gasped. "Wh-what are you doing here?"

Lord Monksleigh laughed. A loud guffaw of a laugh.

"Now come my dear, that is not very friendly. As it happens I am on my way to see your Mama. I suppose you are waiting for that son of mine."

Kate's green eyes flashed and her cheeks reddened.

"I wish you would stay away from Mama," she snapped. "And it is none of your business whom I wait for."

Lord Monksleigh's laugh rang out again, frightening the little squirrel, which leapt quickly to a higher branch of the tree.

"So, Miss High and Mighty! I can see Colin will have trouble with you but I would like to tame you. I enjoy a girl with spirit."

Before Kate was aware of his intention, he had grabbed her shoulders and pushed her back up against the rough bark of the tree and pushed his face close against her cheek. Kate struggled but found she was no match against his strength. She swung her head from side to side, trying to avoid his whisky laden breath.

"How dare you touch me?" Kate gasped. "Let me go at once."

"Not until I have shown you what it is like to be kissed by a real man," he stated, leering down at her.

"Get away from me you brute," screamed Kate, but this only made her molester push her harder against the tree and pin her there with his body, whilst he attempted to hold her still.

"Get away, get away," she screamed, sobbing with fright.

Suddenly Lord Monksleigh was grabbed from behind and thrown unceremoniously to the bottom of the ridge, where he lay looking up at his attacker.

"You heard what the lady said," shouted Tom Fullerton, "so get on your way."

Lord Monksleigh rose to his feet and began to brush leaves and dust from his velvet jacket.

"You will pay for this you churl!" he snarled. "I'll get you hounded out of the village."

"Try it," answered Tom, his fists clenching and unclenching. "If you are not gone in ten seconds I will give you the thrashing you deserve."

Without more ado, Lord Monksleigh turned and hurried back into the wood.

Tom turned to Kate who was sitting crying softly into her 'kerchief.

"Thank you Tom," she cried, "I was so frightened."

Tom took her into his arms and held her quietly until her crying stopped.

"Better now?" he asked.

"I saw what was happening as I came into the field over there," he explained. "So down went my sickle and here I am."

Kate smiled.

"And very pleased I am to see you."

The young couple gazed into each other's eyes and the electricity that Kate had always felt whenever she was near to Tom was now at its strongest. It seemed like hours that they sat there just gazing. They could not look away. That was the moment that they both realised they had fallen in love.

* * * * *

Colin Monksleigh rode happily through the wood towards the disused watermill that marked the boundary of the Hall estate and the Manor land. A few days previously he had received a letter from the priest who had befriended him, offering him a curacy at his church. Since then Colin had spent hours wondering what to do. A few months ago he would not have hesitated to accept the offer but during the past year he had got to know Kate, and the thought of leaving her had caused him much heartache. However, last night he had reached a decision. He would ask Kate if she would consider marrying him. A smile of anticipation lit up his face and he could feel his heart hammering against his rib cage.

The first leaves had fallen from the trees so that they cushioned the sound of his horse's hooves as he emerged from the wood. He glanced up towards the oak tree and what he saw there caused his smile to vanish and his heart to do a complete somersault.

Kate and Tom were standing arms wrapped around each

other. As Colin watched in disbelief Tom bent his head and kissed Kate full and passionately on the lips. Even from where Colin sat motionless on his horse he could see and feel the love that radiated from the young couple. So engrossed were they in their new found happiness that neither heard nor saw Colin turn his horse and ride slowly and sadly back towards the Hall.

* * * * *

Kate and Nella were breaking their fast when the knocker on the heavy oak door rattled loudly.

"Goodness," cried Nella, "who can be calling at this early hour?"

They did not have to wait long for an answer. Seconds later Jed knocked on the door and announced that Sir Colin Monksleigh would like to speak with Mistress Kate.

"My, my," smiled Kate, putting down her cutlery and getting to her feet. "Such formality. Whatever can he want so urgently?"

Kate tripped daintily down the stairs to where Colin was pacing backwards and forwards up and down the hall.

"Colin, my dear friend," she cried. "What has brought you here so early?"

Colin winced as Kate called him 'friend'. Although he knew in his heart that was all he was to her.

"Please, Kate. I need to speak to you privately."

"Oh, of course, Colin. Let us go into father's study."

Opening the door to their right, she preceded him into the room and motioned for him to sit in her father's leather armchair. Colin declined and remained standing.

"Why, Colin?" Kate murmured, her green eyes beginning to register alarm. "You are not at all like the Colin I know. Please tell me what is wrong."

Colin stood gazing at her, taking in her loveliness, the gold of her hair as it hung shawl-like around her slender shoulders, the green eyes and rose-bud mouth. At last he found his voice.

"Kate, Tom has taught me during the past year to be strong

and to face up to what life flings at me and not run away from difficulties like a frightened kitten. Yesterday I almost did run away, but after giving the matter much thought I have come here today to fight for what I love, and whom I love."

Kate stared at him perplexed.

"Colin, my dear, what is wrong?"

Colin crossed the room to where she stood and took her hands in his.

"I must tell you of what I observed yesterday. It is not easy for me," he hesitated a moment. "As I rode from the wood I saw you and Tom in an embrace."

He stopped as he saw Kate's stricken face.

"Oh Colin," she cried, tears glistening in her eyes. "You should have called us, shared our happiness."

Colin shook his head.

"I could not Kate," he said. "I was on my way to ask you to marry me."

"Marry you?" gasped Kate, her eyes wide.

Colin nodded.

"I love you Kate and if you will have me I will learn to run the estate and bring it back to what it used to be. Is there any hope for me my dear?"

Kate looked into his eyes and her lips trembled as she told him.

"Colin I love you as a very dear friend but my heart is given to Tom. I could not marry you and love another man."

"You will never be able to marry Tom. Your parents will never agree to it. Tom is a very good man, but Kate, he is only a working man."

"I know all that. Nella has been warning me for months now not to get too fond of either of you because it would only end in tears." Kate paused looking sadly into his eyes. "I am hoping Father will find a solution when he returns."

Colin put up his hand and gently stroked Kate's soft hair as he told her forlornly, "Kate, there is only one solution to this problem. Marry me and I will hope you can learn to love me in time. Or you must forget both of us."

Kate flinched.

"Oh Colin, how could I possibly forget either of you. We have shared some wonderful times together, such happy times."

Colin walked a few paces away, his chin almost touching his chest so that Kate should not see the distress in his face. Then blinking hard he turned again to face her.

"They have been the best two years of my life," he told her. "But now we are older and we must move on." He looked at Kate imploringly. "You are quite sure there is no hope for me?"

Kate shook her head sadly, tears rolling down her face.

"Dearest Kate do not weep," he whispered, wiping her face on his lace 'kerchief.

"I have been offered a curacy in Norwich so I shall accept that and work hard to make a good priest but we must keep in contact. If things cannot be resolved for you and Tom, then I shall still be there for you. God bless you my dearest."

Colin kissed Kate on her cheek, then rushed to the door and let himself out before she could stop him. Nella found her moments later curled into a ball in her father's chair, sobbing uncontrollably.

* * * * *

The next few weeks passed by uneventfully. Tom and Kate met as and when they could, owing to the harvest which had to be gathered in. Their times together were marred somewhat by the absence of Colin but Kate had received a letter saying that he had settled in well and was enjoying the change in his life. Through Lady Maria Kate learned that Lord Neville Monksleigh was furious at the departure of Colin and was doing his best to find out where he was, so that he could bring him back. Maria questioned Kate as to his whereabouts but Kate was able truthfully to state that she knew not where he was as he had not put his address on her letter.

* * * * *

The harvest finished and the stacks stood golden and tall in the stockyard, their tops covered with plaited straw to keep out the wet. The big barn over at Tom's farm was being decked out in wild flowers and ivy. Trestle tables were placed edge to edge to form one big table and the farmhands' wives were covering the tables with mouth-watering dishes of food. Pies and pasties, roast pheasants and ducks, chickens and rabbits. Wooden bowls piled high with red ripe apples and pears.

It was the custom to celebrate the 'Harvest Home' each year when all was 'safely gathered in'. Each farm in the village took turns to play host and this year the honour fell to Tom Fullerton's farm. Kate had never attended one of these celebrations but this year she had had a special invitation from the senior Tom Fullerton and was excitedly getting ready. Nella was to accompany her as were several of the Manor servants. Kate chose a pale pink cotton dress that was laced at the bodice and Nella had braided her hair and fastened it around her head.

"Quickly, Nella," cried Kate, "it must be time to leave."

"Plenty of time yet," replied Nella, smiling at her charge's excitement, then her hand flew to her mouth and her eyes registered concern.

"What's wrong?" asked Kate.

"My dear, it is the custom to take a thanksgiving present to the feast and I have completely forgotten."

"What can we do? Would Cook have anything?"

Nella shook her head.

"The girls will have taken that."

Suddenly Kate gave a little cry.

"I've solved it," she said, giving Nella a hug.

"We will take two straw baskets and on the way we will gather blackberries and edible fungi."

"Brilliant," cried Nella. "Come along then we must go."

Pausing only to collect a basket each, Nella and Kate hurriedly let themselves out of the kitchen door and set off towards Mill Farm.

In a small thicket by the river Kate was busily picking juicy blackberries whilst Nella search for edible toadstools. Looking up, she put her fingers to her lips and motioned for Kate to bend down behind the brambles.

"What is it Nella?"

"Lord Monksleigh," whispered Nella. "He appears to be heading towards the Manor. Is Lady Maria at home?"

"Yes. She was invited to the Harvest Home but told me it was too 'rustic' for her."

Nella cautiously peeped over the bramble patch.

"Oh good, he is out of sight now. Come along, I'm sure we have gathered enough."

After washing their stained hands in the river they ran over the little bridge and were soon being welcomed by the Fullerton family. Tom's father had been placed in a comfortable chair at the head of the table with his wife standing at his right side. Mrs. Fullerton held out her arms to Kate as her son led her forward.

"Welcome m'dear," she said, a happy smile spreading across her plump brown cheeks.

"We have heard such a lot about you but have only seen you from a distance."

Kate introduced Nella and then Tom instructed everyone to help themselves to the feast. Father Giles Fordham, the parish priest, said a few words of thanks for the successful harvest and reminded all present about the Harvest Service on the following Sunday. After that everyone started on the serious business of eating the tables bare.

The food having just about disappeared the trestles were removed and everyone joined in the dancing led by two elderly men picking out tunes on their flutes. Kate and Tom joined the throng and Nella sat by Mr. Fullerton who regaled her with stories of his youth. Kate noticed that Nella was holding her ear quite often and realised that the noise was getting a little much for her. Shortly after this several of the men, who had been drinking rather too much of the homemade ale, started getting rather ribald and using bad language. Tom was about to have words with them but Kate stopped him saying "No Tom, this is their day. They deserve to be merry. In any case it is time Nella and I started for home. Methinks her head is hurting."

Tom glanced towards Nella and could see that Kate was correct.

"I hate to let you go, my Kate," he said, "but this is getting too rough for you. We will collect Nella and I will see you safely home."

"No, no Tom," Kate protested, "you must stay with your friends."

Tom would not hear of it and in a few moments the three of them were on their way back to the river. At the bridge Nella averted her eyes so that the young couple could enjoy a parting kiss. As Kate and Nella walked towards the Manor chatting happily, they little realised how their lives were about to change.

The yard seemed extremely quiet with most of the servants over at the Harvest Home. Soon the milkmaids would return to milk the cows and the men to feed the other animals. Chickens and ducks scattered before them as they made their way to the kitchen door. Cook, who had not attended the jollifications, saw them approaching and opened the door for them. Her fingers at her lips she 'shushed' them to be quiet, her jolly face for once wore a worried expression.

"Whatever is wrong?" whispered Kate as they stepped down into the kitchen.

Raised voices were heard coming from the room overhead. Kate could pick out Lady Maria's shrill voice and then she heard the deep resonant voice of her father.

"Is that Sir Denzil I hear, Cook?" she asked.

Cook nodded.

"Yes Miss Kate. 'Tis terrible."

Cook took up the corner of her apron and wiped her eyes. Nella gently sat her down in her rocking chair and took her hands into her own.

"Now tell us what the row is about."

"Well it were loike this 'ere," she began hesitantly. "Soon arter you had gone this artenoon, Lord Monksleigh come a ridin' up. He let 'imself in through the kitchen door an' med off inter the hall. I dunt think as 'ow he saw me – cus I was a sittin' in my chair in the corner."

Kate nodded.

"We saw him coming this way." she stated.

"What happened then?" asked Nella gently.

Again Cook wiped her face.

"Ooh it were terrible. It must 'ave bin about an hour later that Sir Denzil cum ridin' inter yard. He took 'is 'orse inter stable an he must 'ave sin 'is Lordship's horse cu 'e cum in 'ere, face nearly purple. 'E kicks off 'is ridin' boots and rushes off into inter the hall and upstairs." Cook stopped for breath for a moment. "Then all 'ell let loose," she went on. "There were a screamin' an' a shreikin' and the men were shouting. Then Lord Monksleigh came rushing through 'ere holding 'is arm – looked like Sir Denzil 'ad caught 'im one with 'is 'orsewhip – an he was wuz shouting that Sir Denzil had not heard the last of this, that he wud git 'is revenge."

Kate and Nella looked at each other in distress.

"I must go to my papa, Nella," cried Kate and ran across the kitchen to the inner door closely followed by Nella. In the main hall Lady Maria and Sir Denzil were still arguing but as Kate and Nella entered they went silent, just eyeing each other belligerently. Lady Maria's face was scarlet with fury.

"Papa, what's wrong?" implored Kate, hanging onto his arm. "Why all this anger?"

Sir Denzil was saved from answering at that moment as Lady Maria's maid came downstairs lugging two heavy canvas bags. Looking at Kate's bewildered face Sir Denzil said softly, "Lady Maria is leaving."

"Leaving? But why? Where are you going Mama?"

Lady Maria gave Kate a vicious glare, her eyes flashing like black steel.

"Mama," she spat out through clenched teeth, "I am not your Mama. Ask him! It's time he told you the truth."

With another frosty glare she followed her maid and the door slammed behind them. They heard the sound of a coach driving away. Sir Denzil turned and looked into the stricken face of his daughter. With brimming eyes and trembling lips she asked, "Papa, if Ma- Maria is not my mother then who is my mother?"

For what seemed an eternity but was actually only a few seconds, father and daughter stared into each other's eyes. Slowly Sir Denzil turned from Kate. A figure stood at the bottom of the staircase holding tightly to the newel post.

"There is your mother Kate," Sir Denzil said gently.

Kate's lovely eyes grew wide with surprise.

"Nella?" she breathed. Sir Denzil nodded.

For seconds no one spoke or moved, and then suddenly Kate and Nella were in each other's arms crying with happiness.

"Now I know why I have always loved you so much," whispered Kate as she wiped away her tears. Then suddenly she began to stagger. Sir Denzil caught her up in his arms and carried her to a settle in his library. Kate continued to tremble and Nella placed cushions behind her back and wrapped a woollen shawl about her shoulders. Sir Denzil looked on with concern not knowing what to do.

"It's alright Denzil. It's the shock. She will be better very soon. Perhaps a little of your brandy would do us all good."

Sir Denzil nodded and fetched the drinks from a tray on one of his desks. Kate, having never tasted brandy before, coughed and spluttered but it soon had effect and she stopped shaking and regained the colour in her cheeks. Sitting up, she motioned to the others to join her on the settle. Sir Denzil and Nella sat down either side of her, each holding one of her hands. Sir Denzil looked at Kate anxiously.

"Do you feel strong enough to hear our sorry story?" he asked.

Kate nodded, squeezing his hand.

"I must know," she said.

Sir Denzil glanced at Nella who smiled permission. Clearing his throat Sir Denzil began.

"It is quite a long story, my dear, and it began almost nine years before you were born. My father had just died and so, of course, the title and Manor and all its land became mine. But I had already become an equerry to King Charles and preferred my life at Court to being a gentleman farmer. As I loved the Manor and the village I did not wish to part with it – my mother had died at my birth and there were no brothers or sisters to look after the estate – I hired a splendid bailiff and he ran the place in my absence. A friend whom I had known since our school days invited me to visit with him at his home in Essex. He was a few years older than me and had married very young. After giving him five children his wife died in childbirth leaving him with a daughter and four young sons. Clifford was at his wits end when he asked me to visit. The boys were quite well behaved children but the daughter was uncontrollable, ready to throw herself at any man, be they servant or nobility. Now he had learnt she was with child."

Sir Denzil stopped for a moment and took a sip of brandy. Then he went on.

"Clifford, being an important member of the Royal Court, could not afford a scandal and had asked me there to see if we could come up with a solution. We discussed the matters late into the night and whether it was due to the wine we had consumed or tiredness, I found myself offering to marry the girl and give the baby my name. The following day I was introduced to Maria." Kate gasped.

"Yes Kate. It was Maria. She was a pretty, dainty girl with sandy coloured hair and I thought to myself that perhaps marriage with her could not be too bad." Sir Denzil sighed. "How wrong I was! We were married in Clifford's private chapel and she came back here to Marley as Lady Maria Ashe. She was only seventeen. Six months later she gave birth to a son and we called him Paul." Kate gasped again.

"So Paul is not my brother?" she queried.

"No dearest, no relation whatsoever." Sir Denzil continued, "After Paul was born Maria forbade me her bed so I kept away from the Manor for long periods. For three or four years Maria seemed to be happy mothering young Paul. Unbeknown to Maria the servants kept me informed of her behaviour! Then she took up her old wanton ways. I had provided her with a personal maid and I found out later that instead of curbing Maria's promiscuity she was encouraging her in it. I threatened to send her home to Clifford, but she had grown used to the lavish life she lived here so she begged forgiveness and promised it would never happen again. I even let her keep her maid! However, to jump on another two years. King Charles asked me to deliver a letter to Sir Wilfred Brokenhall in Suffolk. It was there that I was introduced to Eleanor, governess to Sir Wilfred's children and I was immediately taken with the tall, lovely young women. Call it love at first sight if you wish."

"Just like you and Tom," laughed Nella. Kate threw her arms around Nella and hugged her.

"Go on Papa," she said her eyes shining in anticipation.

"Well fortunately for us, I had an extended stay in Suffolk owing to a sudden spate of bad weather. For three weeks it rained and the local rivers overflowed, so it was six weeks before I could return to London. By then Nella and I had become lovers and spent as much time as possible together. Whenever fate brought me to the east coast I would call to see my love, and you can imagine the agony when Charles sent me off abroad on one of his 'errands'. It was when I returned from one of these foreign visits that Eleanor told me she was with child. I was overjoyed yet at the same time ashamed of my actions."

"I was as much to blame," broke in Nella. "We both knew what the consequences could be."

Sir Denzil smiled tenderly, and then went on. "You see Kate, Nella had no relatives. Sir Wilfred was her guardian, so we thought it best not to tell him until I had an arrangement worked out. I came home to Marley and Maria played right into my hands. Word had reached me that she was still 'entertaining gentlemen' and she had to admit that my informants were correct. I threatened to throw her out and she at once started screaming and weeping and begging me to let her stay. I let her keep it up for a while, then I put a plan to her. Either she did as I asked or she would go.

"You will pretend to your friends that you are with child," I told her – how she had avoided it I do not know, with all the lovers she had taken – "You will tell everyone that you intend going to a relative to have the baby." At first she was furious but when she calmed down she could see a future in it for her. She knew I would be unable to refuse her anything, so she agreed. Six months later I took her to Suffolk to a little nunnery where Eleanor was already in residence. That is where you were born Kate. We waited a few weeks until Eleanor regained her strength and then I brought my family home to Marley. Maria acting the part of the new mother and Eleanor as the wet-nurse and later governess."

Kate looked lovingly at Nella as she asked, "Did you not object to the arrangement Nella?"

Nella smiled. "No dearest, because you see I had complete charge of you. I fed you, bathed you and made all your clothes. Maria only sent for you if one of her friends called and she wanted to play the doting mother."

Kate breathed a sigh of happiness.

"I could never understand why Maria seemed to dislike me. Now it is all crystal clear."

"And do you hate us for what we did?" Sir Denzil asked.

"Hate? Of course not," she answered, drawing them closer to her. "I love you both so much, so much it hurts."

"But what happened this afternoon, Denzil?" Nella asked.

A frown creased Sir Denzil's forehead. "I came home unexpectedly and seeing Lord Monksleigh's horse in the stable I guessed what was going on and caught them red-handed – in bed together! I lashed out with my whip and he grabbed his clothes and fled. Maria started screaming and weeping as usual but this time I took no notice. I gave her an hour to get her things together and get out. Sam the carpenter had not gone to Harvest Home so I paid him to prepare the coach and drive

Maria and her maid to Norwich. She will stay at the Bell Inn tonight and then go to Cromer tomorrow. The rest you know."

Sir Denzil leant back in his chair and drank the rest of his brandy looking very thoughtful. Only the ticking of the clock could be heard for several minutes until he rose to his feet and paced up and down the room, a worried look on his face.

"What is troubling you Papa?" asked Kate with concern.

Sir Denzil turned to face his daughter and Nella.

"Lord Monksleigh," he replied. "He is known to be a vengeful man and I would not put it past him to inform the Parliamentarians of my whereabouts."

Kate gasped and running to her father she threw her arms about him.

"Then you must go," she cried. "Perhaps we could all go. We could go to Holland, Paul would have us I know."

"It is not as easy as that, my dear. There are things to see to here – but it would be a good idea if you and Nella went away for a few days."

"We cannot leave without you Papa."

"Certainly you can," replied Sir Denzil. "A few days by the coast will do you both good. I will give you a letter to give to my friend Sir Henry Attlestone who resides at Winterton. You will enjoy a stay there - and he has a son around your age," he added with a twinkle in his eye.

"I want no other young man but Tom," Kate protested hotly. "Tomorrow I will bring him to meet you and let you see for yourself what a fine person he is."

Sir Denzil looked at Nella, an eyebrow raised questioningly.

"Do I know this Tom?"

"He is young Tom Fullerton," Nella informed him, "from the farm over the river."

"Hmm," breathed Sir Denzil, stroking his beard. "Well bring him to me in the morning and then you must be on your way."

It was a happy Kate who retired to her bed that night although she had niggling worries about her father's safety.

* * * * *

A week later Kate and Nella arrived home from their short holiday to find the Manor strangely quiet and seemingly deserted. They alighted from their hired coach and the driver lifted down their trunks and deposited them down just inside the hall. Then with a bow he leapt up onto his seat and drove away.

"Where can everyone be?" mused Nella.

They did not have long to wait for the answer as almost before she had finished speaking a tumbrel driven by Tom came rumbling round from behind the house, closely followed by Sir Denzil. Both Tom and her father were ecstatically greeted by Kate who was delighted to see her father and Tom together. When all the excitement was over, the questions began.

"Where was everyone?"

"Why was it so quiet?"

Sir Denzil smiled sadly.

"First we must let Tom be on his way," he said "then we will go into the house and I will tell you what I have decided to do. Tom will be back shortly to dine with us." So saying he led the way into the house.

A few hours later they were all seated around the kitchen table waited on by Cook and young Jed. Sir Denzil explained that he had sent the rest of the staff to their homes and that Cook would depart on the morrow. Jed had shaken his head vigorously.

"I will stay with you, Sir," he had said.

Now, the meal eaten, Sir Denzil leaned back in his chair and surveyed the others, who although filled with curiosity, had refrained from asking questions. Kate not able to contain herself any longer suddenly burst out

"Papa! Please tell us what is happening. Why have the servants gone and where are the pictures from the gallery?"

Sir Denzil gave his daughter a sad smile and then began to explain.

"Tom here knows it all," he said. "I have received word from London that my life is in great danger, even more than before and the troops are already on their way here to arrest me and my family. That is why we must leave."

"Tom has been taking the best of the pictures to his farm for safe keeping. Some of the smaller items such as silver, china and books we have taken to the Reverend Fordham to keep until we return."

"Shall we be able to return?" asked Kate tearfully.

"Of course, my dear," her father replied. "That is why I have decided to close the house for a year. The servants have been paid in full for the year so they will not suffer. The cottagers will pay their rent to the vicar. They can also call upon him for help if they are in need. Wherever I go I shall endeavour to keep in touch with Giles."

"But the animals and the farm," cried Kate, "what of them?"

"All taken care of, Kate. Tom will see to the land and help Jim and Jenny with the cattle. You have a fine young man in Tom my dear."

Kate and Tom turned bright red and Kate reached out to squeeze her father's hand.

"I knew you would like him Papa," she said.

Nella, who up to now had not said a word, suddenly got to her feet.

"We must begin to pack if we are to leave tomorrow."

"We must travel light," said Sir Denzil, "only the barest of essentials. We must go on horseback across country to the coast. If we leave in pairs we shall be less conspicuous."

"Pairs, Papa?" There are only three of us!"

"I shall accompany you to the coast," Tom explained. "Once you are safe on board a boat I shall return with the horses."

* * * * *

Kate and Tom left at midday, Sir Denzil and Nella arranging to follow on a few hours later. Kate could not stop the tears that trickled down her lovely face as she looked back at the beautiful old house that she loved so much.

"Do you think I shall ever see it again?" she asked.

"Of course you will," replied Tom fervently. "Once the King and Cromwell have settled their differences you will all be able to come home and everything will be back to normal – anyway you have to come back to me. How can I live without you?"

Kate gave Tom a watery smile, then digging her heels into her horse's flank she led the way across the meadow at a gentle trot. Sir Denzil had told them not to hurry but to go steadily so that onlookers would take them to be a couple out for an afternoon ride.

It was almost night time when they arrived at their destination, a little fishing village a few miles from Yarmouth. Going straight down to the beach they looked around. One or two elderly men sat mending nets and smoking foul smelling pipes. Two younger men were painting an upturned rowing boat with tar. They looked up as Kate and Tom approached.

"Good day," said Tom, "we are looking for a Mr. Wilf Amos. Can you help us please?"

One of the men brushed a mop of greasy hair away from his face, a face bronzed by sea water and sun.

"Uvver ther," he said, "the wun with the green ganzy." He pointed to the group of net menders. Thanking the man, Tom and Kate walked over to where the old men were staring at them curiously.

"I understand you are Mr. Amos," said Tom, addressing the man in the green, fish-stained jersey.

"Thass roite. Oo's askin'?"

"We have a message for you Mr. Amos," Tom said. "Our names don't matter but you can call me Tom. Our message is rather confidential so could you please take us somewhere more private?"

Wilf threw down the net he was holding and after murmuring a few words to the other men he beckoned Kate and Tom to follow him and led the way to a dilapidated shed sheltered from the sea and wind by a grass covered sand dune. Once inside Tom told Wilf that he had been sent by Sir Denzil to ask for his assistance in getting his daughter safely to Holland. Wilf stroked his unshaven chin as he listened to Tom.

Kate stood by the door listening to the lapping sound of the sea as it ebbed and flowed against the shingle on the beach, the gentle shushing of the wind blowing through the marram grass and the raucous cries of seagulls as they swooped overhead. Tears were not far away again as she realised that she would be leaving Tom behind for at least a year. She started as a hand touched her arm.

"It's only me," Tom said with a brief laugh. "You were miles away."

Kate threw her arms around his waist and clung to him sorrowfully.

"I shall be miles away tomorrow and I do not know how I shall be able to abide it."

Tom kissed her tear stained cheek and led her out of the shed.

"Do not fret my dearest one. We have several more hours together yet. Wilf says he cannot sail until first tide tomorrow morning."

"Mek sure you be 'ere by five o'clock," ordered Wilf as he joined them outside. "Tide waits fer no man." With a grin he strode off to rejoin the other men.

"What are we going to do Tom?" Kate asked.

Tom began to lead her from the beach towards a small village.

"We will go to that inn we passed and see if they sell food. After that I will find a room for you spend the night."

"But what about you?" Kate cried.

"Oh I can sleep in the stable with the horses."

Kate did not think much to that idea but not knowing of anything better she kept silent.

The "Lobster Pot" was quite small and seemed to be clean. As it was early evening only a few customers occupied the room, sitting at well-scrubbed tables talking and drinking their beer. Tom and Kate walked towards a couple busily washing pewter tankards. A rosy-cheeked woman looked up and smiled.

"Can we 'elp yer me dears?"

Tom returned her smile.

"We were wondering if we could buy some food Mrs. –er?"

"Miller," she beamed at him, "but called me Dolly – everybody does, and this is me ole man Cecil."

Cecil looked up from his washing and flashed them a toothless grin.

"Young couple need some vittels Cecil. Thass orl roight 'ent it?"

"Corse it is," said Cecil. "I hoop yer loike fish though."

"We love it," smiled Kate, glancing quickly at Tom, who nodded.

"Sit yerselves down then," said Dolly. "It won't be long."

Gratefully the young pair found a table at the far end of the room where a fire was blazing merrily in the inglenook fireplace. They were the recipients of some curious looks at first but as they smiled back at the men they soon lost interest and went back to their own conversations. Very soon Dolly came bustling in carrying two platters of food, complete with knives and spoons, Cecil following on with two tankards of ale.

"There yer be me dearies," she said. "Fish pie. Med it meself only a few hours ago."

"Oh, but Dolly," said Kate hurriedly, "we must not take your dinner."

"Bless yer me dear," Cecil laughed. "There's plenty more. She allus make enough for the hul village."

Placing the foaming tankards before them he followed his wife back towards the bar.

By the time Kate and Tom had partaken of the welcome food and drink, Kate was feeling quite sleepy.

"Come along Kate," smiled Tom. "We will see if Dolly has a spare room for you."

Dolly was happy to oblige saying she always had a room ready for unexpected guests. Tom took out his purse and paid her with some of the money Sir Denzil had given him to see Kate safely aboard the boat. Tom arranged for a four-thirty am call.

Dolly noticing how fatigued Kate looked pointed to a narrow staircase.

"It's the room to the left of the stairs. I hope you an' yer 'usband have a comfortable night."

"Oh, but.." began Tom. Kate grabbed his arm.

"Thank you Dolly, I am sure we shall. Come along dear."

A blushing Tom followed Kate up the staircase.

* * * * *

Nella and Sir Denzil were in Kate's room tidying things away into drawers and cupboards when a clatter of hooves in the yard caused them to halt their activities and an apprehensive look passed between them. Going to the window Nella peered from behind the curtain.

"Soldiers!" she breathed. "Quickly, Denzil, you must go down the secret passage at once."

Sir Denzil shook his head.

"Not without you my dear. Get your cloak whilst I check the front of the house. If we are surrounded by the Parliamentarians we must hide in the passage until they go."

Before Sir Denzil could cross the corridor and enter one of the facing rooms, loud banging on the stout front door was heard. Nella, frightened, grabbed at Sir Denzil's arm.

"You must go at once," she cried. "They will break the door down any moment."

Sir Denzil knew that what Nella said was true.

"But you must come too," he said, "I cannot leave you here."

Nella gave him a watery smile.

"I shall hinder your escape Denzil. Do not worry about me. Once they have gone I will follow on and meet you at the coast."

"But Nella, they will arrest you, they have threatened all my family."

Nella pushed him towards the wardrobe.

"Go" she cried, "I will hold them off for as long as I can. They will take me to be a servant so they will not harm me."

Reluctantly Sir Denzil entered the secret passage and Nella fastened the door behind him. With a thumping heart she picked up a candlestick and had just lit it when the front door opened with a crash. Nella walked to the top of the staircase and stood looking down into the hall. There were at least ten soldiers milling about looking into downstairs rooms, throwing things about and pocketing anything small and valuable.

"How dare you?" Nella shouted down at the men. "How dare you break into this house? What do you want here?"

A big giant of a man, who appeared to be in charge, looked up and saw Nella standing there.

"You, woman, take me to Sir Denzil at once," he ordered.

Nella put a hand to her ear.

"Pardon?"

"Where is your master?" the soldier bellowed.

"I am sorry sir, yer'll 'ave to speak up. I'm very 'ard of 'earing," Nella answered,   trying hard to speak the Norfolk dialect.

"I said – oh never mind. Get upstairs you men and search thoroughly. He must be here somewhere. Monksleigh said he saw him this morning?"

'As we thought,' mused Nella, 'I wonder how much they paid him for his information.'

The soldiers came thundering up the stairs pushing Nella out of the way. Although extremely frightened, she watched as they moved from room to room, searching in and behind every piece of furniture they came across. Her heart leapt into her throat as she saw them enter Kate's room and heard the door of the wardrobe being forced. Holding her breath she waited.

'Please God. Do not let them find the tunnel,' she prayed.

God must have heard her plea because a few moments later the men left the room and went further along the corridor to the suite of rooms once occupied by Lady Maria. It seemed like eternity before the men left the rooms and then split into two parties, some going up the stairs to the attics and servants quarters, the others going downstairs to the kitchens. Tears formed in Nella's eyes as she surveyed the damage done to the beautiful house and its contents. One man had lashed at everything with his sword leaving ugly gashes in furniture and ripping curtains. The man she presumed to be the captain still stood in the hall, impatiently awaiting his men. She looked at his hard featured face only just visible now under his metal helmet. A straggly brown beard covered most of his cheeks and chin.

"Get me something to drink, woman," he called, seeing her looking at him.

"Pardon?"

"Get me a drink, damn you."

Nella shook her head and again motioned to her ear. Thinking that she had better go down before the man became violent, she descended two steps but stopped there as the other men appeared swearing and grumbling.

"No sign of him, Captain," muttered the man with the sword.

The captain swore.

"Then he must be in one of the outbuildings. Search them at once," he shouted.

The men rushed to the kitchen and outside. Nella not knowing what she could do stepped back up onto the top stair and stood looking at the angry captain below.

"Where are the family?" he growled suddenly.

"Pardon sir?"

"I'll give you pardon woman. I said 'Where are the family?'" he bawled loudly.

"Gone sir."

"Gone where?"

Nella noticed that his face and neck, what little she could see of them, were turning decidedly purple and realised that she must not provoke him too much.

"I think I heard Cromer mentioned sir."

The captain was about to question her further but was interrupted by some of his men returning.

"No one about out there sir," one man said, "not even a horse in the stables."

The captain looked up at Nella.

"Which way did Ashe go? If you don't tell me I'll get my men to come up and persuade you."

The man leered at Nella and guffawed loudly. Nella, very frightened now, though trying not to show it, replied with a trembling voice.

"I think he was mekking for Wells. He said there would be boats there."

"Wells?" the captain queried. "Are you sure woman?"

Nella nodded.

"I think thass wot he said, only I can't 'ear proper. It might 'ave bin Lynn or somewhere."

The captain's patience at last snapped. Growling like an animal he turned to his men,

"Get out of here. We'll ride west and maybe we can cut him off. He can't be far ahead."

"What shall we do with the woman sir?" queried a soldier.

"Shoot the bitch," snarled the captain.

A shot rang out. Nella's body crumpled to the floor, the still lighted candle fell from its holder and rolled onto a Persian rug.

* * * * *

Part 3

I screamed! A scream that echoed around the large empty hall and brought Jim running from the kitchen.

"What is it?" he queried, alarm showing on his face.

"It's Caiti," I cried. "She's fainted or something. Can you get some water from the kitchen?"

Jim turned to go just as the servant woman, or whatever she was, appeared in the doorway holding a glass of water. Again I felt that chilly sensation running up my spine. Jim lifted Caiti's head. Taking the water from the strange quiet woman, I put the glass to Caiti's lips. After a few moments she began to stir. She seemed to be mumbling something and I bent down lower to try to catch the words.

"Sebast – Sebastian Thain," she was saying over and over again.

Jim and I exchanged puzzled looks.

"Caiti," I cried, slapping gently on her cheeks, "wake up, please wake up."

"Sebastian Thain," she repeated, as if trying to commit something to memory.

Jim gently shook her and she began to come round. I put the water to her lips once more, and then turned to hand the glass back to the woman. There was no-one there! At last Caiti sat up and looked around.

"What happened?" she asked

"We were looking at that portrait and then suddenly you fainted," I explained.

"What portrait?" asked Jim.

I turned to point. There was no portrait – just a large space where one could have at some time hung! Now I was really frightened.

"Jim let's get out of here. There is something really weird about this place," I cried.

Jim could see my distress and nodded his head in agreement. Helping Caiti to her feet he smiled at us.

"You two wait here and I will nip upstairs and collect the few bits and pieces we brought with us."

Five minutes later the three of us were hurrying down the driveway through the still clinging but thinning mist. Not one of us saw the black clad figure of Nella standing in the doorway, a hand raised in farewell, before she dissolved into the mist. Just before we reached the gateway, Jim opened the car doors with his remote key and we all clambered inside, thankful to be out of that smoky atmosphere.

"Now what do we do?" asked Jim when he had his breath back.

I shook my head but Caiti said firmly.

"We must go back to the village, there are things that need to be explained."

"Talking of explanations," I said, "who is Sebastian Thain?"

"Who?" she queried.

"Sebastian Thain," I explained. "You were murmuring his name as you came out of your faint."

Caiti looked puzzled.

"No idea. I've never heard of him. Something else to ask about in the village."

During our conversation Jim had been fiddling with the buttons on the car's dashboard. Suddenly the radio came on full blast, making us all jump.

"Nothing wrong with the battery then," he remarked. "I'll see if she starts."

With the first press of the starter the engine throbbed into life.

"Well, I'm blessed," laughed Jim. "I wonder what happened to it last night?"

Caiti picked up her mobile phone from where she had flung it. Pressing in the correct digits for Tom's mobile, Caiti laughed when she heard the ringing tone and shortly afterwards Tom's voice.

"Oh Tom," she cried, "we've had such a mysterious night. Can you spare an hour or two? I must tell you about it! We are about to come back to the village now the car has started."

"What do you mean the car has started? Have you been broken down?"

"All will be explained shortly," Caiti told him. "It's very early. Can you manage to meet us?"

Tom explained that the milking had been done and he could meet us at the Riverside Inn very soon.

A happy Caiti put away her mobile. Jim tried to back the car onto the road but one of the wheels was stuck in a rut so we had to get out and help him manhandle it. We soon had it free but it was facing the wrong way.

"Can I get my cardigan out of the boot before you start up again Jim? It's rather

Nippy," I said.

Jim said he would get it out and went to the boot. My cardigan had got screwed up under the picnic hamper so before giving it to me he gave it a good shake, not noticing that a handkerchief that had been up my sleeve had fallen out and blown across the grass verge and onto a bramble hedge. Minutes later we were on our way back to Marley Ash. The mist had gradually disappeared and the sun appeared low on the horizon as we pulled up outside the inn. Soon Tom's Land Rover appeared and Caiti flew into his arms. We watched them talking animatedly together for a few moments before we walked over to join them.

"Whatever is Caiti trying to tell me?" Tom laughingly asked. "What is all this about a fog and the car stopping?"

"It's true, Tom," Jim answered, "we suddenly drove into this thick black fog and the car refused to go any further, even the mobiles stopped working."

"Gracious me," exclaimed Tom. "So what did you do? Did you spend the night in the car?"

"No," I replied, "we had stopped by some large gates so guessed there must be a house. We thought there would have been a phone we could use to call you – but- oh Tom, it was scary."

Tom's face was registering all kinds of emotion - disbelief, sympathy and more.

"Where were you when all this happened?"

"About a mile along Primrose Lane," Jim answered.

Tom's eyebrows went up swiftly, almost to his hairline. He looked at us incredulously, mouth open.

"But there is no house anywhere along Primrose Lane," he said at last. "Look we'd better go into the pub and sort this out. Caiti looks in need of a drink as I'm sure you are. Have you had anything to eat?"

"Not since last night," I informed him. "There was no-one at home, just a maid, or housekeeper, dressed in very old fashioned clothes. She fed us and showed us to rooms where we spent the night."

As I was speaking we had entered the little inn and we all sat down. Gladly!

Tom left for a few moments to go into the kitchen, where we heard him speaking to his sister. When he returned we resumed our strange story and his face grew even more incredulous.

"Well, all I can think," he said when we had all finished, "is that you took the wrong lane."

"But we didn't," Caiti hastily broke in, "we saw the signpost quite clearly. One minute the sun was shining, the next we were in thick fog."

Tom put his arm about Caiti's shoulders and gave her a hug. "I don't disbelieve you, but it's just so puzzling. After you have eaten we will go for ride and try to find this mysterious house."

Just then Fiona came in carrying a tray containing three steaming bowls of porridge and mugs of tea.

"There's bacon, eggs and toast to follow," she said.

We thanked her gratefully and she went back to the kitchen from whence we could smell the wonderful aroma of bacon. As we ate Tom excused himself and we saw him run across the green and enter one of the cottages. When he returned later he had with him Joe and Ted. Luckily we had finished eating as we had to recount the story once again. The old men listened politely but I saw by their faces that they took us for a trio of loonies. Caiti had left the table and was studying one of the pictures on the walls. Suddenly she gave a cry and we all turned to her startled.

"Here it is," she cried, green eyes sparkling, "here is the house!"

We all went over and looked at the painting. It was not very big but it showed a lovely rose garden and in the background was a house, clearly Elizabethan because of its E-shape.

"Yes," I cried. "That's it. Tom, now where is it?"

Tom shook his head.

"I've no idea. What about you Joe? Ted? Do you recognise it?"

Joe slowly took out his spectacles, put them on and peered at the picture. Ted did likewise.

"No," said Joe at long last. "Nowt loike thet round 'ere. Is there Ted?"

Ted shook his head. I had an idea.

"Is it signed anywhere Tom? Perhaps that would give us a clue?"

Tom carefully lifted down the picture and studied the bottom corners.

"There is something here," he said excitedly, "but some of it is hidden under the frame."

"Is it possible to remove the frame without doing any damage to it?" Jim asked.

Tom called Fiona.

"You're the artist. What can you tell us about this?"

Fiona studied the little painting.

"It's certainly very old. If the backing is disturbed it would probably disintegrate."

"Can you read the signature?" Tom asked.

Fiona nodded.

"All that is visible. I can see a small 'e', then Ashe and the date 1646."

Tom and Jim whistled and I said "Phew". Caiti carried on looking at the pictures.

"Where did you get these pictures?" she asked.

"They've always been there as long as I can remember," answered Tom. "There are other similar ones in the attic at the farmhouse. The only up-to-date ones here are the pictures painted by Fiona."

Caiti turned to look at me, a beaming smile lighting up her face.

"Look at this Meg," she cried excitedly. I went over to where she was pointing.

"You remember when we visited the farm yesterday and I looked up to the ridge by the river?"

I nodded mystified.

"I said something was missing. Here is proof. Look at this old painting. There is a watermill by the tree." She moved further to her right. "Now look at this one painted by Fiona. It is exactly the same view – but no watermill."

Tom's face was quite a picture.

"B-but there hasn't been a mill there since I was born," he said. "Can you remember one Ted?"

Ted shook his head.

"Not in my toime."

I had been studying the pictures carefully and suddenly realised that they were the ones that we had seen in the strange house. When I informed the others of this fact, I could see by their faces that only Caiti believed me. Even Jim looked sceptical. Caiti was now concentrating on another picture. A portrait of a bearded gentleman dressed in a dark velvet jacket with a lace collar and long black hair. I was astounded at Caiti's demeanour. She seemed to be stroking the man's beard and her lovely green eyes were filled with tears. She was murmuring something, but her voice was too soft for me to hear the words.

I realised she was in one of her trances. I caught one word "Papa".

"Caiti," I cried, urgently tugging at her arm. "Come away from there, something is upsetting you."

Tom crossed the room to her side and took her into his arms. She pressed her face against his chest and he gently stroked her hair.

"What is it, darling?" he queried. "Who has upset you?"

For a moment Caiti did not stir, then suddenly she raised her head and smiled at Tom and she was back to her old self once again.

"Tom," she cried excitedly, "you have the answer to all your money problems hanging around you. These paintings are worth a fortune. This one I am sure is a Van Dyck." She pointed to the portrait of the bearded man. "There could be others."

Tom and Fiona looked at each other in amazement.

"I did think there was something special about that portrait," exclaimed Fiona, "but I had no idea that it was a Van Dyck! How could it have got here?"

This caused a great deal of speculation, each one of us coming up with different explanations. My theory was that they had been given to one of Tom's ancestors by the owners of the house we had seen.

"Ah yes – the house!" grinned Tom. "We'd best be going. I'll just give Dad a ring to tell him what we're doing while you hop into the Landroverover."

Ten minutes later we were bowling along the country lane packed tightly in Tom's vehicle. Joe and Ted included, determined not to be left out.

"Are you sure this is the way you came?" Tom asked as he turned into Primrose Lane.

"Positive," a trio of voices assured him.

There was no fog now and I was enjoying the scenery as we travelled along. So many different greens in the hedgerow, so many wild flowers growing on the verges. Wild parsley and campions, Old Man's Beard festooned bramble bushes. How peaceful it all looked now, completely different from earlier. Suddenly Tom's voice jolted me from my reverie.

"Can you see it yet?"

There was no house in sight! Tom kept driving and Jim, Caiti and I kept a lookout for anything familiar. Suddenly I felt that icy cold feeling that I had experienced the evening before.

"It's here somewhere," I cried.

Tom stopped the engine of the Landrover and we all stepped out. There were no gates, no house. Nothing but a field full of thistles, brambles and long grass.

"Are you sure this is where you stopped?" Tom asked.

"Well it was so thick. The fog was so black and smoky that it is hard to tell where we were," answered Jim, "but if Meg says it was here then here it was because she gets these intuitions and she's never wrong."

Caiti had moved a few yards further along and suddenly she called out.

"Here! Here is where the car got stuck. Look! The ruts the wheels made are quite clear."

We joined her to examine them and then I discovered my handkerchief fluttering in the gentle breeze and fastened down by thorns.

"See!" I cried jubilantly, "more proof that we were here."

"Well there's certainly no house here – never has been that I know of," remarked a puzzled Tom.

A thought struck me and turning to Ted and Joe I asked, "What did you mean yesterday when you told us not to go down Primrose Lane? You said something about it being haunted."

The old men looked at each other rather sheepishly.

"How is it haunted then?" I persisted.

"Well, thass loike this 'ere," Ted began, "several people roundabouts rekun they 'eve sin a lady dressed in black, walking the lane as if she is lookin' fer suffin or sumwun."

"An' it's allus when it's misty," added Joe.

"And do you believe in ghosts Ted?" asked Jim

"Dunno but there is suffin funny down 'ere. Trevor George

wot farms oover the road 'e 'ad a funny thing happen 'ere. Be the year afore last. 'E wor cumin along on 'is ole tractor on 'is way hoom arter ploughing the fild wots behind us. It was getting' leart so it wuz a bit dull an 'e wuz gooin faster'n whut 'e should, when this 'ere woman walked right out in front on 'im."

Ted stopped for breath so Joe took over.

"Cor 'e nearla 'ad an heart attack. 'E stopped the tractor 'an jumped down roighte quick – but there wuz no sign of 'er. No blood – narthin. 'E searched the 'edgerows buth sides of the road. No sign of anywun. My word 'e wuz suffin sceered. 'Is missus reckon 'e wuz as white as a sheet when 'e got hoom. They told the pleeceman but 'e onla larfed, thort Trevor 'ad drunk too much of 'is 'ome med wine."

"An' thass not all," added Ted, "this 'ere fild wot's all thistles and brambles, there's summat wrong with it. They call it the Witches Blight hereabouts 'cus narthin exept what yer see will grow onnit. Last September toime ther wuz a crop of gret big ole blackberries on them brambles and sum of the ole mawthers frum the village came an' picked baskets of um ter mek inter jam an jelly."

Ted stopped and looked me straight in the eye.

"Yer might not believe me, missus," he went on. "Not one jar would set. They tried puttin' in more apples with it, even rhubub but narthin warked so it all got tipped out. Ent thet roighte Tom?"

Tom and Caiti were standing hand in hand, listening with amusement to the old men's stories.

"Yes I must admit that is quite true, Meg. Fiona and Jean were two of the women who tried it. No one had ever known anything like it before. If it had been October they would have blamed the Devil as he is supposed to walk over brambles in October. Anyway this field has been like this for generations. Nothing at all does well on it. I remember my grandfather telling me that his father had ploughed it up and set a crop of wheat. The crop failed so he tried again with turnips. They rotted before they could be lifted. It was left to fallow for a year and then they tried putting a flock of sheep on it. They got foot-rot!" Tom laughed. "So since then we have left it alone."

"I don't blame you," Jim laughingly remarked. "Shall we walk across it, see if anything gives us a clue as to what happened last night?"

Skirting round the prickly brambles and carefully stepping over the thistles we slowly made our way across the field. We must have walked at least half a mile when I realised the icy feeling that I had experienced earlier had gone and was now replaced by a warm, happy sensation.

"Something strange has happened to me," I told the others, explaining how I had felt. They then admitted that they too had noticed the cold, sombre atmosphere as we had entered the field.

"And has it gone now?" I enquired. They all admitted that it had.

"Do you feel warm and unafraid now?"

They nodded. Caiti turned to us and smiled.

"Things will grow again now. It has been exorcised. There never have been evil spirits around here, just puzzled, unhappy ones."

"Caiti, how do you know such things?" asked Jim, startled.

"I just do, Jim. It's because I'm psychic."

The others all laughed but I knew there was something different about Caiti and wondered if my own intuitions came from the same source. After all, we were related!

Still walking and chatting we covered at least another mile, then suddenly we came to a ridge and ascending it we looked down, and there, in front of us, were the river and lovely fields. Fields of all shades of gold and green. Barley, golden and almost ready to harvest, and acres of peas and beans. A small oak wood was a short distance to our left with one solitary tree standing alone to our right. This was the tree Caiti had pointed out to me when we'd visited the Fullerton farm yesterday! I could see the farm in the distance with the river almost circling it as if it was being cradled in watery arms. Noticing that Joe, Ted and Jim had stopped and were now sitting on the grassy bank, I walked over to the tree and sat down on one of its protruding mossy roots. Tom and Caiti were a little way apart from me, their arms now wrapped around each other. Not wishing to spy on them I closed my eyes but this did not prevent me hearing their conversation.

"Isn't this just beautiful?" Caiti breathed.

Tom agreed. I heard them kiss. Then Tom spoke again in a puzzled kind of voice.

"You know Caiti, I only met you yesterday but I feel that I have been here before, just like this, holding you in my arms, but it's not possible!"

"Yes, Tom, it is possible. Look down at the river. Empty your mind and concentrate on the water. Now what do you see?"

There was silence for a few moments and then Tom spoke haltingly, as if in a dream.

"I see a raft, there's a girl sitting on it, it's you Caiti! There are two boys pulling the raft along. One must be me because of his hair, the other one I cannot remember – oh yes, it's coming. Colin, that's his name."

I had opened my eyes to look at the river while Tom was speaking. There was only water flowing gently past! Caiti and Tom still stood holding each other tightly. I dare not speak in case I did something to damage them. It was clear that they were in a different life, a different dimension. Then they moved and the spell was broken. Seeing me by the tree they walked over.

"Do you believe in reincarnation Meg?" Tom asked me.

"I do now," I answered.

It was as we were going back across the field that I stumbled over a lump of something sticking up in the grass. Picking it up I could see it was mud encrusted wood. Rubbing at it I got most of the dirt off and I was left holding a little bird, slightly smoke damaged, but otherwise perfect. I held it out to show the others. Caiti took it into her cupped hands and gazed at it.

"It's the little sparrow," she said softly.

* * * * *

When we arrived back at Marley Ashe the village had become alive with people going about their business of the day. The children had already left for their schools, the mothers with younger children spending a few minutes chatting together at their gateways. An Eastern Counties bus was standing at the bus stop outside the church, the driver waiting patiently for an elderly lady to count out her change for the fare. The postman was delivering mail to the Inn as we pulled up.

"Anything interesting Harold?" called Tom

"Not unless you call junk mail interesting," replied Harold. "Better luck tomorrow."

With a cheery wave of his hand he mounted his cycle and rode off to the next pair of cottages.

"All I git these days is funeral plans and sorter rubbish," grumbled Ted.

"You had better go in and ask Fiona to cook you a bit of breakfast," Tom said laughing. "Your poor old legs must be aching with all the walking we've been doing."

Ted and Joe needed no further telling and disappeared into the pub.

"What do we do now?" Jim asked. "We still haven't discovered who this Sebastian Thain is."

"No," replied Tom. "Somehow the name is familiar but I can't think where I have seen it."

"I have a strange feeling that the church may hold the answer," I remarked.

"One of your famous instincts?" laughed Jim

"Maybe, anyway it's worth a try."

We set off across the green, leaving Tom to phone his father to ascertain if his help was imperative. When he joined us he informed us that old Tom had given him the day off. We decided to start in the graveyard and look at the names on the old stones. Luckily the grass had recently been mowed except for a patch at the back of the church, which Tom explained was kept as a conservation area. We searched diligently but came up with nothing until Jim gave a shout.

"Over here," he called. "This looks like a Thain family plot."

We rushed over to where he was studying a grave-stone.

"There doesn't seem to be a Sebastian though."

There were eight memorials to the Thain family. Two of them were so badly corroded that they were unreadable but the others we could just make out after poking out the moss etc. that had formed in the names over the years. Jim was right – no Sebastian! I could see that Caiti was disappointed.

"Don't give up yet Caiti," I said. "Let's try inside the church. Do you have a key Tom?"

"The key is in the porch," he answered and led us round from the graveyard and into the porch where he retrieved the large black key from a niche high up in the wall. Inserting the key into the lock, he turned it and with a loud groan the heavy oak door slowly opened.

The church was not particularly large but was attractive and looked well cared for. It had a centre aisle with very ancient pews on either side and consisted of a naïve and a small sanctuary. The carved stone font stood just inside the door. The aisle was covered with a slightly faded blue carpet that ended at the bottom of two steps which led up to the altar. The reredos behind the lace clad altar was beautifully carved with figures of birds and animals peeping from and around an apple tree under which stood the figures of Adam and Eve. I could clearly tell it was Adam and Eve because Eve held an apple in her hand and Adam had a snake wrapped around his body. Pointing it out to Jim I remarked that it was the most beautiful piece of carving I had ever seen. Jim agreed. Tom told us there was a brass plaque on the wall nearby saying that the reredos was carved by a man named Frederick Shaw in 1660 after the previous one had been destroyed during the Civil War. He was also responsible for restoring the poppy heads on the pews. Caiti, I noticed, was still clutching the little wooden bird that I had found. Her eyes took on that glassy far away look as she held it up towards the reredos and we all noticed that one of the birds depicted was identical to the one she held.

"There, Freddy," she said, "I still have Betty's bird." Reverently she laid it down upon the altar, turned to us, blinked once or twice and was with us once more.

"Let's start by looking at the memorials on the walls," she said. " Sebastian might be up there."

There were quite a few plaques, some really old stone ones, and some newer ones in brass. Nowhere was there one to Sebastian Thain.

"There seem to be several to a family named Ashe," remarked Jim. "They must have been an important family here at one time. There's a slab down here on the floor to a Sir Edward Ashe and his wife Lady Barbara."

Caiti sat down on a pew, a beaming smile upon her face. Turning her radiant face up to Tom, she told us…. "Ashe was my family's name for generations but Great, Great Grandfather had no sons so the name died out. Oh Tom, isn't it exciting? This village is where my roots lie and now I know why I have felt all along that I belong here."

Caiti jumped up and flinging her arms about Tom she kissed him passionately upon his lips.

"Steady, Caiti," I cautioned, "you have no proof. Ashe is not an uncommon name."

"I just feel it in my bones," she laughed, "but come on, we still have this Thain man to sort out."

We covered all the walls, even got on hands and knees to read an inscription on the bottom of the brass lectern. No luck there either.

Feeling slightly despondent, we sat down in the pews wondering what we could do next. It was so quiet, nothing to be heard but the song of a blackbird somewhere outside. I sat gazing at the colourful windows, watching as the rays of sunshine caught the colours and reflected them into a myriad of jewels upon the white washed walls.

"I've got it!" Jim suddenly shouted, shattering a quietness and making us all jump.

"Gracious, Jim," I said alarmed. "You almost gave us a heart attack."

"Sorry," he replied laughingly, "but I have had an idea about that altar."

"What is it then?" asked Caiti eagerly.

"Well …," Jim began, pausing for dramatic effect. "Why is the altar raised like it is? I believe there is a vault under it."

"You mean like the one at Terrington?" I asked.

"Exactly! Now if there is a vault, there has to be a door somewhere. Any ideas Tom?"

Tom shook his head.

"I've never heard of one."

"The entrance to the one at Terrington is outside," I remarked. "Could this one be as well?"

"We'll have a look while you two look around in here."

So saying Caiti pulled Tom to his feet and disappeared outside leaving Jim and I to crawl about around the altar steps looking for possible clues. A short while later they came back shaking their heads.

"No trace of a door out there," Tom said shrugging his shoulders. "No sign of one being bricked up either."

"Oh dear," I sighed. "Back to square one!"

We stood silently looking at the altar for a few moments searching for inspiration.

"Perhaps we're looking for Sebastian in the wrong place," said Tom. "Maybe he's somewhere else in the village."

"The pub?" queried Jim.

"No," I answered, "he is here somewhere I just feel it."

"What about the church registers?" asked Jim. "Perhaps they could……"

Jim was interrupted by Caiti's excited cry.

" Have any of you moved the sparrow since I put it on the altar?" she asked. Wonderingly we shook our heads.

"Well take a look at it. When I placed it here, it was facing towards us, now it's facing the reredos." Caiti went to study the reredos more closely.

"Must have been a draught," suggested Tom. "Perhaps when we went outside to look for a door."

Caiti called us over.

"Look! The sparrow is looking at his double on the carving. If you feel around it carefully it seems to be in a kind of recess. None of the other birds or animals is."

We all took turns to examine it and found out that what she said was true.

"It's like a knob," I said wonderingly. "Try turning it Tom."

Tom took the bird into his hand and gently turned it. Feeling a slight movement he turned it again, this time a bit harder and miracle of miracles, part of the reredos moved forward with a tremendous creak. Unfortunately the altar prevented it from opening for more than about four inches but we knew we had found the door to the vault. Caiti and I were almost crying with excitement. Tom and Jim were shaking hands and clapping each other on the shoulder. Tom caught Caiti by the waist and swung her around in a circle. Eventually we all calmed down.

"Well, we've found the vault," said Jim. "Now we have to move the altar to be able to get to it."

"Yes we have found the vault thanks to our friend the little sparrow," I remarked. We turned to look at him. He was facing us again!

"But we still don't know if we have found Sebastian," said Tom. "Or why we have to."

Tom looked at his watch.

"Well I suggest we go over to the pub for something to eat. We cannot move the altar without more help so come on, let's leave it for now."

Carefully locking the door to the church and pocketing the key, Tom led the way across the green, a bubbly Caiti by his side. Jim and I followed on smiling bemusedly at each other.

"Wish I had a woodworker like that Frederick Shaw," remarked a grinning Jim. "We'd be millionaires in no time."

"And pigs might fly," I laughed.

It seemed like hours before we got back to the church. None of us could eat much – we were so excited, but a nice cool drink was very acceptable. We had to wait until Tom had rounded up a couple of helpers. One of them was Fiona's boyfriend and the other was a man called Mervyn who happened to come to deliver some crates of beer from the brewery, just at the right time to get roped in. Ted and Joe, not to be left out, brought up the rear. Fiona had armed Caiti and me with cobweb brushes and dusters and the men were carrying various tools and torches. We were prepared for all eventualities.

Firstly, I removed the lace edged cloth from the altar and carefully folded it before laying it down in a pew. Caiti had taken the little wooden bird and now sat it on the cloth. The four men grasped the ends of the altar and on Tom's count of three they lifted it about three feet from the reredos. The door, although very stiff, opened to its full capacity revealing steps going down. Tom turned to his two extra helpers and thanked them.

"You can get back to your delivery now," he told Mervyn, slipping him a fiver for his trouble.

"Not likely," he replied. "I want to see what's down there. Never seen anything like this afore."

Tom laughed.

"None of us have. What a wonderful craftsman that Frederick must have been."

Tom turned his powerful torch and shone it down the steps. Fiona was right. Hundreds of years of cobwebs and grime met our eyes. Caiti, impatient as ever, moved forward and started brushing at the tangle, causing dust to fly and make us cough.

"Steady on, Caiti," I cried. "Now we will have to wait until it settles."

"Sorry," she giggled.

Moments later Tom descended the steps and looked around him.

"You can come down now," he called. "It's not too dirty. Bring the other torches though because there is no light."

We went down very gingerly, not quite knowing what to expect. It was a bit cramped when all eight of us had reached the bottom. The four younger men had to stoop slightly as the roof was quite low. Now the torches were all on we could look around us. The room was completely bare except for a coffin resting on a stone plinth in the centre of the floor. We could see a nameplate on the side of the coffin but not clear enough to read it. I stepped forward with my duster and quickly rubbed at the plate. Not daring to look I told Caiti to read it. We all held our breath.

"It's him," she cried. "It's Sebastian Thain."

We cheered and clapped. Even Mervyn the lorry driver, who had no idea what all the excitement was about, felt involved and joined in. When we had all quietened down a bit Tom suddenly raised his free hand and shushed us.

"We have forgotten where we are," he said. "We are in someone's burial place and so we must respect that and act with a bit of decorum."

We glanced at each other shamefacedly and stood silently.

"It's alright," Tom continued, "I was making as much noise as anyone but we'd better be quieter from now on. So we've found Sebastian. What do we do now?"

Standing in a circle around the coffin we looked about us. There was nothing else in the room. Jim turned to Tom.

"I think we have to open the coffin."

Tom agreed and held his torch so that he could see how the lid was fastened down. The coffin was made of solid oak but we could see that the lid was beginning to crack open due to age.

"We need something to prize it up," Tom remarked.

"Should we be doing this?" I asked apprehensively. "Caiti, how do you feel about it?"

"We must," she replied. "There has to be a reason behind all this."

Fiona's boyfriend, John, had gone up the steps and was soon down again carrying a tyre lever and some strong screwdrivers.

"You are quite happy about this all of you?" Tom enquired.

"Positive," answered Caiti.

The men set to work and Caiti and I stood back out of their way, Ted and Joe with us. Soon most of the lid was off and Tom and Jim shone their torches into the coffin. Tom raised his head and looked at us.

"It's full of books and bundles of papers," he told us.

"Is that all?" queried Mervyn. "I thought it might be full of gold or silver."

Tom laughed.

"We should be so lucky."

"Well, I'm pleased you've found something anyway but I'd better get across the green and unload the crates before I have my boss after me."

"I'll come and help you," said John.

"Well thanks again for your help," said Tom. "We'll give you an update on what's happened next time you call."

Mervyn and John departed leaving us to lift out the books. It was a tricky occupation as their ancient leather bindings were beginning to crack open. We took them one by one and placed them on a pew in the church. The papers turned out to be old documents and several bundles of letters. These were extremely brittle. Once all these were removed we discovered several linen bags and a square box. Jim opened one bag and was startled to find that it contained silver ornaments. Once the contents of the coffin were safely carried into the church we looked about to see if there was anything that would explain our strange find.

"Maybe the books will tell us," said Caiti. "I can't wait to have a look at them."

"All in good time," laughed Tom.

"Was there a date on that coffin?" I asked.

"No. Nothing but the name," replied Tom. "I wonder what happened to his body?"

It was decided that we would get the books etc. over to the inn where we could see them better. We shut the door to the vault and made for the exit each carrying a precious bundle.

"What's behind that velvet curtain?" Caiti asked.

"That's the bell ringing tower," explained Tom.

Caiti laid her books down and pulled aside the curtain. Two bell ropes dangled through a hole in the loft but Caiti's eyes were drawn to a stone plaque on the wall. It was a list of all the past vicars dating from 1520.

"What is it Caiti?" I asked. "What's so interesting?"

"That name," she murmured. "Colin Leigh. I know I should recognise it but it's not quite right."

Looking at the list of names I read - Colin Leigh. Vicar 1656 to 1680.

"Come along," I urged her. "Let's get these books over the green. The men have already gone."

It was difficult to close the door behind us but we managed it and trotted off to join the others.

The books proved to be fascinating. Fiona let us use their private sitting room so that we should not be disturbed by customers, and we settled down to try to decipher them.

"Where on earth do we start?" asked Jim.

"Let's see what they are first," Tom replied, picking up the book nearest him. For a few moments he studied the contents then looked up at us. "This seems to be the missing parish register of births, deaths and marriages," he said. "Our vicar has always said that there appeared to be several years missing in the Church Registers. This one is dated from 1600," he turned to the last entry, "to 1650." Tom put the register to one side and looked at the other three books. "These appear to be private journals or diaries as we call them. These two are written by Giles Fordham, priest, but this one does not give a name. We shall have to try to read it to find the author."

"That will take some doing," I remarked. "That spidery old English writing and spelling has got me beat."

Tom and Caiti turned their attention to the letters. Carefully tied in bundles with ribbon, now rotten with age, they began to fall apart as soon as touched. The first and smallest bundle was written from an address in Norwich and was written by a Colin Monksleigh.

"That's it," cried Caiti, "you remember, Meg? I said the name on the plaque was familiar but not quite right."

"You did," I agreed, "but earlier when we were on that river bank Tom mentioned a Colin. Could he have been the writer of these letters?"

Tom and Caiti looked at each other thoughtfully. I was quite expecting one or both of them to go into a trance but the moment was broken by Fiona bringing in a tray of cool drinks. "We will read them later," he said. "Wonder who these are from?" he carefully smoothed out the parchment and gasped.

"What is it?" we asked.

"These letters are from Holland," he explained, "and the signature is Catherine Ashe."

Caiti almost snatched them from him.

"Let me see," she demanded. Silently she read the first letter, screwing up eyes as some of the words eluded her. Eventually she said "This letter to the priest is asking for news of her mama and papa who she says should have followed her to Holland but have not arrived. She also asks as to the welfare of Tom Fullerton Esq."

This caused us all to laugh, all except Jim, who had been flicking over the pages of the priest's second journal, and now seemed immersed into what he was reading. He looked up at us, a smile lighting up his face. "I've found it," he declared. "The house," he went on as we looked mystified. "This entry states that "DA has collected his horse and has ridden away instructing me to give his second horse to Miss Eleanor Marsh when she arrives. She did not arrive. Later that evening I saw flames coming from the direction of Marley Manor and, thinking that it was a haystack, paid no heed. I was horrified to find on the morrow that the Manor had been completely burned down and a female form had been discovered in the debris. God rest her soul.""

We looked at each other, relieved that we now knew that there had once been a house but horrified at what had happened to that poor woman.

"The Lady in Black," muttered Tom. "But I'm still mystified. I've heard of ghosts but never a ghost house."

"Well you have now," I told him, smiling. "At least you know we didn't imagine it."

Caiti was sitting very quietly, her face pale and drawn, a far away expression in her green eyes. Tom noticed and putting his hand on hers enquired if she was ok. Caiti nodded.

"Let's see what is in this bundle of letters," she told him.

The ribbon broke as Tom went to untie it and the letters scattered over the table, some disintegrating completely so proved unreadable. A few remained more or less intact and Tom picked up one and looked for the signature. "There is no signature," he said. Looking at the letter he read it to himself and then looked at us one by one, lastly at Caiti who was waiting, wide-eyed, for whatever news he had to tell.

"This has apparently been smuggled out of the Tower of London. Whoever wrote this was captured by Parliamentarians just before he reached the safety of the coast," he paused, "he wishes the priest to inform his two dearest loves as to his whereabouts. Obviously this priest was a great friend of the writer and knew to whom he referred." Tom picked up the next letter dated two months later. "He says in this that he is not allowed to receive or send out mail but a young boy helps him by smuggling out his letters and getting them to a friend, who in turns passes them on. He is worrying about his two ladies and hopes they are safe." Tom pushed the letters neatly to one side. "We will read the rest later," he said.

Caiti had picked up another letter written by Catherine Ashe and was reading the faint writing. Soon tears were rolling down her cheeks.

"Whatever is wrong, my darling?" cried Tom, putting his arms around the sobbing girl and holding her close. I took the letter she was holding and quickly scanned through it.

"The poor girl," I murmured, handing the letter over to Jim.

Catherine had written to the priest.

"My dear friend and confidante, I know not how to impart this news to you. I am to be wed very soon. Paul lost his wife last year in childbirth and he is to marry me to hide the disgrace he says I have brought upon the family. Lady Maria's words me thinks! If I cannot wed my beloved Tom, I care not what happens to me. Please, my kind friend, inform Tom that he is my only love and whatever life has in store for me, I shall love him till I die. The child we have created will be loved and cherished. Lady Maria told me cruelly what had happened to my darling Mama and that Papa is in the Tower, sentenced to death. I pray he may be spared. Your prayers and forgiveness for the sins I have committed are asked for.

Catherine Ashe."

Dropping the letter with the others, Jim sat with his head in his hands for a moment.

"You know, Meg. I feel as if I knew these people," he said.

Caiti had recovered from her weeping and when I asked if she would like to take a break from the papers, she told me to carry on. Jim picked up one of the documents and unrolled it. It was a record of the birth of Denzil Thomas Ashe. The date just nine months after Catherine had sailed for Holland. Tom collected the letters etc. into a neat pile leaving just the journals.

"I think that we shall find everything we need to know in these journals," he said, "What do you say if I take them home, read them and mark all the relevant parts? It will be much easier that way." As we were all weary and hungry we were glad to agree.

"Can't we just see what is inside the box?" asked Caiti.

"Very well," replied Tom and opened the wooden box only to find a smaller box inside. This box opened with a hinge and we all craned our necks to see what it contained. We gasped as Tom lifted out a gold casket.

"Is that real gold?" Jim asked astounded.

"Looks like it, Jim," Tom said. "There is an inscription on the side. Let's see what it says." Tom read the inscription, his jaw dropped and then he placed it on the table so that we could all read it.

THIS CASKET CONTAINS THE HEART OF SIR DENZIL ASHE, BENEFACTOR OF THIS VILLAGE.

We sat staring open-mouthed in total silence. Fiona, coming in to remove the drinks tray, commented that we looked like a shoal of fish. After we had explained she looked rather shocked.

"You must take that back into the church at once," she cried. "You have desecrated that poor man's resting place. What will the vicar say?"

"Don't suppose that he knows that there is a vault," remarked Tom, "but you are right Fiona, we must take the casket back. When the vicar returns from his holiday I'll ask him to reconsecrate it." We all agreed. Jim had been sitting looking at the casket deep in thought. "Penny for them Jim," I said, nudging his arm. He jumped.

"I've been thinking," he told us. "The "DA" the priest mentions in his journal must be Sir Denzil Ashe, so Catherine over in Holland must be his daughter. The lady who died in the fire was her mother, so where is she buried? Surely there is a monument or something to her. They must have been influential in the neighbourhood so someone would have given her a decent burial."

"Perhaps the journals will tell us," commented Tom. "There are quite a lot of loose ends to tie up."

"I'm going to have another look at those old pictures," stated Caiti and strode off into the inn dining room. We followed, it being close to dinner time.

The men decided to go outside for a breath of fresh air so I joined Caiti at the pictures. Even I as a novice at art could see that some of them could be quite valuable. Caiti was concentrating on one particular picture. It was a family portrait showing a bearded man and a lady dressed in Royalist clothing with their children, a boy of about twelve and a pretty little girl who looked to be about four. A small brass plate named them as Lord Denzil and Lady Maria Ashe and their children Paul and Catherine. I spotted another portrait nearby showing the same little girl sitting on the lap of an attractive young lady. This one had an inscription embossed into the oak frame. It read "Catherine and Eleanor."

"That's queer," I muttered to myself but Caiti heard.

"What is it?" she asked.

"Well take a look at this picture and then at the one you have been studying. If you remember in the letter you read to us earlier, Catherine said she was to marry Paul. If Paul was her brother she could not possibly marry him. There is a mystery here somewhere, and then in this picture Catherine is with Eleanor. Caiti I am positive that this is the woman at the house, the one you called Nella. If so, she was the one burnt in the fire."

Caiti agreed that it was indeed Nella and we decided to curb our impatience until all the journals and letters had been studied. Dinner over, the men took the casket back to the church, replaced it within the coffin and after closing the reredos door, pushed the altar tight up against it.

There was a feeling of anti-climax during the evening. Caiti went off to the farm with Tom, taking all the books and papers with them, so Jim suggested we had a stroll around the village. He seemed to be in a very thoughtful frame of mind. Several times I spoke but he seemed not to hear. At the empty vicarage he suddenly stopped and stood gazing at it. It was an attractive building, early Victorian I thought to myself. The front was almost covered by Virginia Creeper and rambling roses, pretty pink ones that I could smell from where we stood. Tom had told us that no one lived there now but someone had mown the lawn and the flower beds were reasonably tidy.

"How would you like to live there?" Jim's voice coming so unexpectedly made me jump and I had to ask him to repeat his question being not quite sure that I had heard him correctly. "I asked if you would like to live there. We've always said we'd like to buy an old house in the country and from the outside this looks perfect."

I agreed but had reservations.

"There could be dry rot or woodworm," I remarked, "and I don't suppose there's a damp proof course and anyway it's too far from your business."

"I am a builder, remember," laughed Jim. "It cannot be too bad because the last vicar and his family only moved out nine months ago. A few of my men could get this transformed in a few weeks. As for the business I can run that from here. All it takes is a good manager and a loyal staff. I could even start up another branch around here." Jim put his arms around me. "Just think," he went on, "we are still young. We can expand. After all R.G. Cater had to start somewhere!"

Laughing, I agreed to think about it. We continued our stroll, Jim pointing out all the empty properties and suggesting how they could be converted into other uses. "I will have a talk with Tom senior tomorrow sometime," he said, his voice alive with anticipation.

"We really must go home tomorrow," I told him trying to calm his excitement, "we all need some clean clothes and your men will be wondering what on earth we are doing." Jim smiled. "It's less than an hour's drive home. We can hear what Tom and Caiti have discovered and then I will tell the Fullertons my suggestions on how to improve the village."

"They haven't the money for alterations yet."

"They will have if they agree to my first plan." Jim refused to enlighten me further so as it was becoming dusk we made our way back to the inn where we were putting up for the night. Caiti was staying at the farm.

It was getting on for eleven o'clock the next day before Tom and Caiti put in an appearance.

"Sorry folks," Tom apologised, "had some farm chores to see to before we could get away."

"Duty before pleasure," Jim laughed. "Well, how did you get on?"

"Brilliantly," they chorused. "We've got it all sorted out," said Caiti. "It's all very interesting but so sad."

As it was such a beautiful day we sat on the grass in front of the inn. Tom had the journals before him and I saw that he had put in several paper markers.

"It is mainly the story of the Ashe family, although there are quite a lot of other items not relevant to us." He opened the book at the first marker. "This entry explains the relationship that was puzzling you Meg," he began. "Apparently Sir Denzil went to see the priest shortly after Catherine was born and confessed to him that Eleanor was the child's real mother and that Lady Maria was only pretending to be the mother. This was because when she married Sir Denzil she was already pregnant by another man and Sir Denzil married her to save a scandal as her father was a great friend of his. Her son was born and they called him Paul. Sir Denzil loved him as if he had been his own. It was six years later when he met Eleanor and they fell in love. Paul was eight when Catherine was born and they grew up believing they were brother and sister."

"Oh," I gasped, "so they were not related?"

"No," Tom answered. "There are a lot more details here which you can read later on." He flicked over some pages. "These entries are all about the Civil War. Sir Denzil being a Royalist went off to London to be with King Charles, some of the estate staff going with him. Others joined the Roundheads, leaving only the very young and the very old to run the farm and the Manor House," he paused. "One man to join Cromwell's forces was a Tom Fullerton, from Mill Farm. This farm was one of several in the area owned by Sir Denzil and rented out to tenant farmers."

"So he must have been an ancestor of yours, Tom" Jim remarked.

"Seems like it," Tom replied. "Looks as if we go back a long way. Anyhow, during the battle of Naseby, this Tom was badly injured and had to have his leg amputated. His young son, also Tom, then had to run the farm so was saved from fighting. He supported neither side."

"So history is more or less repeating itself," commented Jim. "What with you having to come home to help your father."

Tom nodded, then went on.

"There are several mentions of a Lord Monksleigh who, it seems, was a compulsive gambler and womaniser. It seems he was a regular visitor to Marley Manor during Sir Denzil's absences. His eldest son, Colin, wished to become a priest much to his father's disgust. Colin often visited Giles Fordham to discuss his problems. Eventually he left home and went to Norwich to become a curate, changing his name to Colin Leigh."

"Then he must have become the priest here some years later according to the plaque in the bell tower, Caiti," I said smiling.

"I hope he was happy," she remarked sadly, one of her far away expressions crossing her face.

Tom turned a few more pages.

"These entries tell of the hardships endured by the poor people of the parish owing to the continual forays by the Roundheads. Crops spoilt, animals killed and the church damaged both inside and out. Sir Denzil left money with Catherine to help the villagers and Giles remarks more than once that Catherine and her father were well loved by all. Then comes the entry which explains some of the letters we have already read. After Lord Monksleigh had reported Sir Denzil's whereabouts to the Roundheads, Sir Denzil was forced to close up the Manor, send servants home and with the help of the young Tom Fullerton removed some of his valuable silverware into Giles' keeping, Tom taking the pictures to hide at the farm. Tom accompanied Catherine to the coast and saw her safely on board a boat sailing for Holland. Sir Denzil had to flee hurriedly leaving Eleanor to follow on but as we already know she was unable to do so."

Caiti took up the story.

"It gets really sad from now on," she told us. "You have seen the letters from Catherine about her distress. In some of the other letters she asks why Tom has not written to her as she has sent him several letters and has had no reply. In the journal Giles Fordham says that Tom Fullerton is broken-hearted because he has heard nothing from Catherine although he has written several letters to her. Obviously someone was keeping back their correspondence. The Lady Maria no doubt! The next entry of importance is one telling of the beheading of King Charles in 1649 and the repercussions and disgust felt throughout the country as a whole. Cromwell formed his own Commonwealth and more and more Royalists lost their lands and in many cases, their heads. It was soon after the death of King Charles that Giles heard of the death of Sir Denzil Ashe. He too was beheaded and his body buried in a rough grave somewhere just outside the Tower. The villagers were bereft and mourned for many weeks. It was during this time that they decided to add Ashe to the name Marley in remembrance of him."

"Ah," ejaculated Jim, "so that is how the village was named."

"Yes Jim," Tom replied. "It has always puzzled people. Everyone thought it was named after a tree but there is not one ash tree around for miles."

"Obviously the "e" on the end has got lost over the years," I remarked.

Tom agreed.

"Now we know the truth we will have a new sign made and Ash will become Ashe again?"

We all nodded our agreement, then, I remembered something.

"We still haven't learnt where Sebastian Thain fits into all this."

"We are now coming to that, Meg," Tom said with a grin. "It seems that after Sir Denzil died some of his friends in London discovered where he had been buried. With the help of his young friend they were able to remove the remains and he was taken to a nearby churchyard and given a Christian burial. His heart they had placed in an unmarked casket, the gold casket which we found in the church. Several of his friends had clubbed together to buy this, but the next problem was how to get it back home to Norfolk! As it happened one of Sir Denzil's servants was a member of the Thain family and he thought up a scheme to hoodwink the Parliamentarians should they get suspicious. They had already discovered that Sir Denzil's body had been removed and were searching any conveyance heading for Norfolk. Sebastian had a coffin made and several holes were bored into it to let in air. One of the well-to-do friends had a large carriage in which the coffin could rest and still leave room for someone to accompany it. One foggy morning Sebastian climbed into the coffin, the casket placed between his legs, the shroud put in place and the lid fastened on. They were several miles from

London by the time the fog cleared and except for four or five times being stopped by soldiers who demanded to see inside the coffin, they made good time to Marley."

"They prevented the soldiers from opening the coffin by telling them that Sebastian had died from cholera," put in Caiti, laughing.

"A messenger had been sent on ahead to warn Giles Fordham of what was happening so that when the coffin arrived it was taken straight into the church and Sebastian was freed," Tom said.

"I'll bet he was ready for a drink!" Jim said grinning.

"Except he had something to eat and drink in there with him," I remarked.

"Must have had," said Tom. "Anyway, the coffin containing the gold casket was placed in the vault and Giles put the letters and other documents in the coffin, adding to them as they arrived. The inscription on the casket was added later."

"Does he say what happened to Sebastian?" asked Jim

"Yes, Jim. It appears he had married a girl in London, so after visiting his relations here he took the horse and carriage back to London."

"A brave young man," stated Caiti. "Are there any Thains around here now, Tom?"

"There is Keith Thain and his family living in Mill Lane and a few scattered around in other villages nearby."

"Is there any more information?" asked Jim.

"Ah yeah," replied Tom. "Quite important information regarding our family – Oh! Before I go on to that, there is one last letter from Catherine. She writes to say that after her son Denzil was born, she and Paul sailed to America to try their luck at growing flax and setting up a factory to make linen. That is the last we heard of her."

"I hope she was happy," said Caiti sadly.

"Is there any news of Tom Fullerton?" I asked quickly, noticing her stricken face.

"Not in the journal Meg," answered Tom, but in the church

138

register there is an entry recording the marriage between Thomas Fullerton and Rebecca Hendry. He was thirty nine years old and she was twenty two, and in the births it is recorded that their first child was a girl named Catherine and then a son named Thomas."

"And so it went on through the years," Jim said.

"Now what is the news about your family?" I asked.

Tom threw back his red gold head and laughed.

"You'll never credit it," he chuckled. "As you know after King Charles I was beheaded, Cromwell formed a Protectorate and reigned for several years. Well, he began giving land which he had taken from Royalist families to men who had fought with him during the Civil War. Because Tom Fullerton had lost a leg in his cause he was given all the property owned by Sir Denzil Ashe. So, from owning only thirty acres he became the owner of everything as far as the eye can see, and further."

"So Catherine and Paul were left with nothing," I stated. "What a terrible man that Cromwell must have been, oh, I've just thought? That is why your farm, or should I say estate, is called Oliver's Gift."

"That's right, so another mystery was solved last night, but Meg, Cromwell was not really a wicked man. He became so overcome with religion and where King Charles believed strongly in the Catholic faith so Oliver Cromwell believed in the Protestant cause. Anyway Meg, he can't have been truly bad because he had quite a few connections with Norfolk. His grand-daughters lived and died in Yarmouth."

I had to laugh because they all knew how I felt about our lovely county. If strangers come and settle in Norfolk and love it as I do they are very welcome but woe betide those who start to find fault. As far as I am concerned they can pack their bags and return from whence they came!

We realised at this point that we were hungry so made our way back to the inn where Fiona served us another splendid meal. As we sat slowly sipping our coffee, Jim told Tom that he would like to talk to his father about an idea he had had which would benefit the village. Tom said he would take us to the farm after the evening milking was done and everyone would be free. He would call a family meeting.

"You do realise that we shall have to go home after the meeting, don't you Caiti? You have to fly back to Australia on Friday and we have to get your clothes washed and packed before then."

I watched as Caiti's face first turned white and then a rosy pink. She turned to Tom and their arms wrapped around each other.

"I'm not going home," she said softly.

Jim and I stared at them, our mouths agape.

"N-Not going home Caiti? Whatever do you mean?" I gasped.

"Just that. Tom and I are going to get married."

"But Caiti," Jim exclaimed, " you have only known each other for a few hours, how can you possibly know you want to get married?"

"We have waited nearly four hundred years to marry – this time it *will* happen, as soon as we can get the banns read."

I could see there was no use arguing with her so informed her that she must ring her folk in Australia at once to let them know what she intended doing. Tom said he must get back to the farm; there were several jobs he had to see to. He asked Jim and me to go with them but I declined as I felt I must go back for another look around the churchyard.

Tom told us if we felt like a row up the river we were welcome to use his boat which was tied up under the willow trees. We thanked him and waved as they drove off, promising to come and pick us up later.

Jim was a bit reluctant to go back to the churchyard but when I told him I had another intuition he readily accompanied me.

I made my way to the conservation area and picking my way through masses of daisies and poppies, not to mention nettles, I

140

looked around and there right beside the wall that enclosed the churchyard I found what I was looking for, a flat granite slab. Jim joined me as I stood looking down at it.

"What is it?" he asked.

Bending down I pushed the flowers and greenery to one side and could see something cut into the granite. Scratching out the dirt with a bit of stick we just read one word.

NELLA

"Clever girl!" he murmured. "What made you think of looking here?"

"Well I knew she must be buried somewhere," I answered. "Then the feeling came that it must be in the oldest part of the churchyard. If you look at the dates on the graves over there they are much later." I pointed to the tidy part of the graveyard.

"By the look of the old stones leaning against the church wall they must be re-using the ground," he replied.

" Look," I said quickly, " there is something else written here, right at the bottom."

Together we cleaned out the moss until we could read the words.

SOON TO BE UNITED IN HEAVEN. DENZIL

"How sad," I remarked, feeling tears pricking at my eyelids. "But how could he have paid for this when he was shut up in the Tower?"

"Mmm – well we know Sir Denzil left a lot of his valuables with the priest – perhaps he left money too. Maybe when he heard of Nella's death, he got a message to Giles Fordham and asked him to see to things for him."

"That must be it, anyway that seems to be the last bit of the jigsaw in place so what do you say we find that boat for an hour or so?"

* * * * *

The boat was tied up where Tom had told us, under the canopy of willow trees. It was so cool there after the blazing sunshine.

141

Even the resident ducks were sitting on the bank preening their feathers and paid no attention to us. Jim picked up the oars and after a few false starts – including one where he dropped an oar and almost toppled us overboard trying to retrieve it – we were away. After a few minutes we were out of the shade and into the sun once more and I wished I had brought my sunhat. Jim said his arms ached and asked if I would take an oar. It was a hilarious few minutes before we got settled and between us we turned the boat around and set off for the welcome shade of the willows. Putting the oars in the bottom of the boat, Jim suddenly grabbed me round the waist and kissed my surprised face.

"Come on Meg, how about a cuddle?"

"Don't be daft, someone might see."

"So what! We are married you know."

"There's a time and a place for everything," I laughed. "Even the ducks have their beady eyes on you. You'll have to wait till we get home."

"Is that a promise?"

"Probably."

Playfully slapping at his hand now squeezing my knee, I jumped from the boat.

"Come on, let's get a long, cold drink," I urged and hand in hand we went into the inn.

* * * * *

The meeting was a great success. Fiona, leaving Jean in charge of the inn for an hour or so, joined us, so there were seven of us around the table. Jim began by telling Tom senior that he had been noticing all the work that needed doing on the houses around the green. Tom agreed but as Tom junior had told us, there was very little money to spend on them. Then Jim dropped his bombshell.

"I think I have found a way to help you out," he stated, "that's if you agree to my plan."

Everyone turned towards Jim, anticipation showing on their faces.

"Would you consider selling me the land you call Witches Blight?" he asked.

For what seemed a long moment no one spoke. Each of them, including me, completely astonished.

"I know you want to keep this land for your family," Jim went on, "but if Caiti married Tom, then Meg and I will be a small part of your family. I have been in touch with my bank manager and can offer you a good price for the land." Jim named a considerable amount, causing us to gasp.

"But what would you do with it?" Fiona asked. "Nothing will grow there."

"Houses will," replied Jim. "The village needs new life and this is what I propose to do if you all agree to let me buy it."

Smiling he took a sheet of notepaper from his jacket pocket and laid it on the table.

"This is a plan of what I would like to do."

I noticed that Tom senior was looking just a little dubious but the others seemed quite interested. Jim pointed to his plan, saying with a grin at me,

"Of course this is only a rough sketch drawn up last night when Meg was fast asleep, but I think it is feasible. As you can see it is the shape of a cloverleaf. A road will run straight up the centre then form a loop. The houses around the loop will be four bedroom executive type houses with plenty of room between them and the gardens front and back. The bottom two loops or leaves, if you like, would be three bedroom houses and either side of the road before it reaches the bottom loops could be two bedroom starter homes for young couples."

Jim looked around at all their faces waiting to see how his proposal had gone down. Tom senior's brows were drawn together but he was quietly studying Jim's sketch.

"Well, I don't know what you others think but I think it's a splendid idea. That field has been nothing but a millstone round our necks for generations." This came from Tom's young brother.

"What do you think, Dad?" asked Fiona.

Tom senior leaned back in his chair and looked at his wife.

"Well," he began slowly, "are you sure it would work? It would double the amount of the people in the village but would they be content to stay? Except for the inn, there is nothing for anyone to do. There is no school and no shops. No, I doubt anyone would want to live here."

"Oh Dad," Fiona cried, "it's a lovely place to live and once we have renovated the cottages and the inn, it will be very attractive."

Her mother agreed and she turned to her husband.

"Tom, you have always said you would like to convert the old mill into holiday homes but could not afford to. Well here is your chance."

"That's a great idea," Jim said excitedly. "I noticed there are two derelict cottages by the side of the river. Do those up, convert the mill and advertise fishing holidays."

"The money won't spread to all that," Tom senior grumbled.

"Yes, it will Tom," Jim said eagerly, "Meg and I would love to live here in this village and we think we have found our ideal house."

Five pairs of eyes swivelled in our direction.

"The redundant vicarage," I informed them. "That's if you have no plans for it."

They all shook their heads.

"Then would you consider selling it or if not, would you rent it to us?" Jim asked.

They all looked again at Tom senior, who once again was looking dubious.

"Oh go on Dad," urged Fiona, "it will only start to decay if it's left unoccupied, and I for one would love to have Meg and Jim as neighbours. Jim seems full of bright ideas that would benefit us all."

Jim laughed.

"I haven't done yet," he said. "Why not start a farm shop? That would bring in people from other villages. Everyone likes fresh fruit and vegetables and you have several people in cottages who must have a surplus of these every year. You could sell your eggs and even flowers. There's no end to it!"

Everyone laughed.

"We could make chutney and jam and pickles and oh Mum, why ever haven't we thought of that before?" cried an excited Fiona.

"Is there anything else?" Tom asked grinning.

"Yes, a very important idea which will appeal to you Fiona." Fiona's eyebrows rose.

"Me?" she asked.

"Yes," Jim told her. "You must start an art gallery! First of all, the very valuable pictures should go to auction and the money you get from them will enable you to build an extension to the inn. You can show your pictures in there, even do some framing."

"Hang on," broke in Tom junior, "surely those pictures belong to Caiti. They would have been passed down through her family if history had been different. In fact everything we own should have belonged to Caiti."

"No, no," cried Caiti, "way back in Tom and Catherine's days, if a girl had any inheritance when she married it automatically became her husband's property. So you see, if Catherine had married Tom then everything would have become his. The village would have been owned by the Fullertons whether or not Oliver Cromwell had anything to do with it. So get the pictures valued, sell the silver and make the village a beauty spot."

The outburst by Caiti caused quite a bit of discussion but we could all see her point.

"Didn't you say you had more pictures here in the loft?" I asked. "May we see them?"

Young Tom and his brother said they would get them and left the room. The rest of us chatted about this and that, discussing other ways we might bring life and money into the village until the two young men returned bearing at least twenty pictures. Fiona fetched a duster from the kitchen and carefully dusted the wrappings before undoing them. There were at least two other Van Dycks and other artists that we knew.

"We must get a good valuer to take a look at them," Fiona said. "Some of these must be worth millions."

The atmosphere in the cosy farmhouse became electric, so much excitement being generated. Then I remembered something.

"Tom," I said, "is there another picture somewhere, a rather large one?"

Tom nodded.

"Yes," he said. "It is so big I have no idea how they got it up there in the first place."

"Let's see if three of us can manage it," suggested Jim, rising to his feet.

It took nearly twenty minutes before they could manoeuvre it through a trap door in the hall ceiling, but with a bit of pushing and twisting there it was on the dining room table.

Again Fiona dusted the wrappings before undoing them.

"To prevent dust getting on to the paint," she explained, seeing our puzzled faces.

We all held our breath as the portrait was revealed. I wondered if it would have the same effect on Caiti as it had when we saw it in situ in the Manor but no, she had tears in her lovely green eyes as she gazed once more on the beautiful girl in the portrait. Tom put his arm around her waist and I noticed tears glistening on his eyelashes. We looked upon the portrait in awe. Two girls, identical twins, but born well over three hundred years apart. Caiti and Catherine! Catherine and Caiti!

The spell was broken by Fiona, who studying the signature declared the portrait was worth a fortune. "This man was a pupil of Van Dyck but went on to become equally as famous," she told us.

"Wherever are you going to hang that?" asked Paul.

We all laughed.

"We'll find somewhere, won't we darling?" Caiti answered. "I do know that I shall never part with it." Tom agreed with her.

"Put four legs on it and it would make a very unusual coffee table," grinned Paul.

"Enough of your nonsense, young man," laughed Tom, "or you'll find yourself with four legs, across your back more than likely."

"Ooh, spare me, sire," cried Paul. "Mercy, I beg of you."

The room echoed with our laughter. Jim took my arm as he looked at Tom senior.

"Well, Tom," Jim said, "we must go and leave you to your deliberations. I'll give you a ring tomorrow to see what you've decided."

"No need," said Tom senior. "I have made up my mind. You can buy the land and the house once I have had someone to value it. You and Meg will be an asset to the village."

There were a few moments of kissing and back slapping and then Jim drove us away from the farmhouse and the village of Marley Ashe.

EPILOGUE

Three years on and I am sitting on a bench on the village green, a darling little girl crawling on the grass beside me. My little girl! What a surprise for Jim and I. Married ten years and nothing had happened then within a few months of us living here in Marley Ashe I found I was pregnant. Jim says it must be something in the air.

What a different village it is now! All the houses Jim's firm built are occupied. The cottages around the green have been renovated and painted. The Riverside Inn has been repaired inside and out and a glossy new sign hangs proudly over the door. To my right stands the village sign, beautifully carved by one of the village men. On one side it shows the Church and the Inn, on the other side is a Royalist shaking hands with a Puritan, these painted by Fiona and the sign stands on a plinth made of Norfolk flint. We now have a Wives' Club which is held fortnightly, there is a Youth Club held in a converted stable behind our house and a Toddler group run by Mavis Grant, one of the newcomers. The Church congregation has doubled much to the Vicar's delight! Tomorrow we are to have a "Knock out" on the green. Four villages have promised to send a team. Jim, Paul and John are all in our team.

Last year we had a wonderful service when the Bishop came and re-consecrated the vault under the altar. We had had it all cleaned up and painted. A purple velvet cloth was placed over the stone plinth and the Bishop placed the gold casket on the top and blessed it. Caiti gave the portrait of Sir Denzil to the Church and it was hung on the wall. Everyone present at the service was allowed to view the vault and then it was closed secretly and the altar pushed up against the reredos.

Tom senior and Marie his wife have retired from the farm and have now taken over the inn. Fiona married her John last year and now lives in one of the renovated cottages by the green. Her Art Gallery is a great success, several local artists showing their work there and this draws people into the inn, so much so that Marie has had to take on more staff.

The Farm Shop is flourishing giving Ted and Joe a new lease of life. Every inch of their back gardens are set with all kinds of fruit and vegetables and when they are not busy on their own plots they can be seen helping out in some of their neighbours' gardens. Mrs. Dennis, in one of the new houses, used to be a cook in a large town house and makes mouth-watering cakes and pastries to sell. Another young woman knits and crochets so it has become something of a cottage industry. They sell their goods, just giving a small percentage of each sale to Jean, who is in charge of the Farm cum Craft shop. Jim has set up a builder's yard and office in a redundant Methodist Chapel on the Norwich Road and is getting quite a bit of work in this area now.

Caiti and Tom, after their marriage, set up home at the farm and Paul, not wishing to be a gooseberry, had two rooms converted into a comfortable bachelor pad – for the time being anyway! So everything is faring well for the village. The new houses are situated on the new road which the family christened "Denzil Drive", so much nicer than Witches Blight we thought!

Caiti called to see me a short time ago, bringing some splendid news. She had just come back from the Norfolk and Norwich Hospital where she had gone for a scan. She is now expecting the next little Tom to inhabit "Oliver's Gift".

THE END

Lightning Source UK Ltd.
Milton Keynes UK
UKOW06f0817271015

261461UK00009B/120/P

9 781909 908932